Entertaining a Shadow
A Novella

KHALILAH YASMIN

For Love, Muses, & Consciousness

TABLE OF CONTENTS

CHAPTER: 8 BALL

I can hear the loud buzz of the helicopters above searching for my body. If you're reading this, I have died. I'm writing this from the grave or wherever they decided to place my ashes. I imagine that I was cremated. I sure hope so at least. I had plans for my ashes. All plans seemed to manifest, ... eventually.

There I was standing in handcuffs as a helicopter flew overhead, with a spotlight on myself, and an eclectic group of others. The night was dark and chilly. The only thing I could hear was my inner monologue with God and my heartbeat as it pound through my entire being. My flesh was vibrating violently. I watched the tear induced snot from the girl next to me blow in the wind at the same rhythm as the palm trees ahead of me. I knew it was time to wake the fuck up. NOW.

"Dear God, I know you're watching right now," I stated inside of my head as an array of voices bounced around in the background. "If you get me out of this situation, I promise to use the gift you gave me and tell my story. Also not to touch another drug again. Please help me," my inner monologue conversation with God was concluded.

Earlier:

I knew the moment I arrived at this BBQ that I wasn't supposed to be there. I was on the phone with my best friend before I went in, trying to talk myself out of going. But I was kind of a loner. They had food. I brought food. I like food. It was a win-win.

I wanted to be nice to my drug dealer whom had been a reliable source in Las Vegas following an event when I decided to use drugs to numb my thoughts.

"FRONT DOOR," the automated voice on the door alarm system stated each time a guest entered the home of my dealer. The air was painted with the best marijuana Las Vegas had to offer. I had other plans that night so didn't want to lose focus by participating in Mary Jane's allure. The computed door alarm foreshadowed a voice that would join us later that evening.

I stared at the long table of the lavish home adorned with a smorgasbord of every drug imagined. There was a rainbow assortment laid out upon the table as if they were chips, salsa, and ribs. Like a psychedelic drug infused barbecue. Everything was up for grabs. This already made me nervous. That and that damned voice of the front door alarm.

I was having the same conversation with myself on repeat, "Zosia, what are you doing here? GO."

Obviously I did not listen.

"Zosh, take a hit. You might as well. You're still here," Joey stated passing me the professionally rolled joint. I thought about it for a moment and decided to live a little. Living was something I had to fit in when I could... So I did.

Women were walking around the house wearing everything from swimsuits to red bottom Loubitins in their fancy Vegas dresses. Some of them nude. Me? I was wearing something comfortable and purple. Little did I know 'Purple' would be part of my description later. I followed someone's Pomeranian puppy into the living room. 'Mean Girls' was on and a group of men were watching it.

"You don't party much do you," a dark skinned Black male stated whom had been quiet most of the evening. "Not really. How can you tell," I asked placing a pillow in my lap to hold onto because I was that fucking stoned. "You just don't strike me as the type to do anything reckless," he responded with a stoic face as others laughed in the kitchen engaged in their own conversations.

"So you're calling me a square," I said, squeezing the pillow as more guests entered the lavish home.

"No, I'm not calling you a square at all. I just can tell," the gentleman said as he sat in a chair separated from the crowd. "What about you? Why aren't you smoking or drinking... or anything for that matter," I asked inquisitively as I observed the mental state of everyone except HIM.

"I have a drug test next week. I probably shouldn't even be here. Just like you," he said as he turned his head back into the television.

"I don't like the feeling of marijuana. I can't drive to my next location like this," I stated to myself as I daydreamed about the 8 ball in the front seat of my car. I felt like it had the potential to bring me back level. So I sat and stiffened my body up, preparing to leave so that I could bury my head into my lap and sniff the dusty white goodness. That's when I heard it. The voice that shook the high all the way out of me.

"THIS IS THE LAS VEGAS SWAT TEAM. COME OUT WITH YOUR HANDS UP."

How can I describe how I felt in that moment other than fucked? Though I was not guilty of distributing anything and had just purchased the largest amount of cocaine I have ever had in my possession, I was innocent right? I was a good girl. I used to be a square. Frank Ocean sang about 'Nova-cane' and how numb it made him feel on the night I decided to do the same.
I wanted to numb my memories and my disappointments.

It helped, temporarily.

I was the first one out of the house. On the outside I appeared calm. On the inside, I was screaming like a little bitch. "PURPLE SHIRT. HANDS BEHIND YOUR BACK," a SWAT TEAM member stated as I walked slowing in his direction. They were wearing all black and I was blinded with the lights above me and in front of me. I could imagine the frantic chaos in the house behind me as I walked towards my destiny. I imagined Joey running from his backyard into the barren desert. Neighbors were watching from their doors with shock that I could see on their faces in the darkness.

The swat team member placed handcuffs on me as other girls came running out of the house in tears. I met eyes with one of them and saw the despair in her face. Her despair seemed to ask why I was so calm. I had to be calm. That's all I knew.

We were then placed standing facing the SWAT truck and I saw Joey come out of the house, in the corners of my eye. I began to wonder if he knew this drug raid was going to happen and had purposely invited all of his customers to his home. While I began to get angry, I showed no emotion. I was angry with myself.

I didn't trust my intuition when I had been on the phone with my best friend Jane earlier that day. Jane had no idea that cocaine was my best friend in her absence. Jane had never tried anything of the sort and thought very highly of me. She also had a notion that cocaine made people angry and mean. I used to try to tell her that wasn't true. I wanted to tell her that those people she knew in the past that did cocaine and were horrible, were just horrible.

But by telling her that, I would also have to reveal how I knew this for fact. I would have to tell her that I recently read during my Psychology class, that Sigmund Freud explored cocaine and found it had magical effects. I would have to tell her that during my studies, I decided to do my own research and found that this methamphetamine helped me focus and finish my schoolwork while also numbing the things in my past that hurt me. When would I get to tell her how much I loved her? I was in handcuffs.

"I didn't do anything wrong," one of the girls sobbed as a SWAT officer advised her to stop talking. I was the only Black person there so if my face were filled with the blood of emotion, no one would know. Her face however was scarlet red on the dark desert night. She was showing what I was feeling on the inside. DESPERATION.

They placed us on the sidewalk, side by side and asked for our car keys. My heart stopped.
I had an 8 ball of cocaine in the front seat of my car that modeling had afforded me. I was petrified but I refused to tell a lie. That's my motto. Always has been. What is meant to be is going to either happen or it is not.

I handed over my keys and imagined the worst possible scenarios. I saw jail. I saw being forced into being someone's personal sex slave in jail. I saw my dreams shattering before me. I saw my face on the news and them ironically using one of my best modeling photos where I'm smiling innocently. Who would my one phone call be? I needed three phone calls. Maybe four.

They never found the 8 Ball in the front seat of my car that night. And if they did, they didn't care. They brought me my keys and told me I was free to go. God allowed me to tell my story... and so I shall.

CHAPTER: SHADOWS

I adapted an alternate reality; a place I went to when things hurt or got too bad. I became someone else. She was another side of me. She enabled me to do things that the other me would not do. I guess you can say she lived out the hurt. It was like I turned off and someone else turned on.

Usually all it took to switch was someone to say something or do something that made me feel something I did not want to feel. Other times, she came to do things that I wanted to feel… even if only temporarily. She never lasted longer than an hour. She would often disappear in the midst of the experiences she placed me into. The other me would emerge like a curtain was lifted from my face. Changes were subtle to most people as they only look with their eyes, but they couldn't see my mind when my inner characters began to intervene in the outer world.

CHAPTER: INCUBUS

According to the legend found in many old scripts such as mythology and the bible, an Incubus is a male demon that seduces women during their slumber. The opposite of an Incubus is the female demon, Succubus that has sex with men as they slumber. Variations of their existence have described these demons with shape shifting capabilities in order to successfully fool their prey by pretending to be human. Some of these demons find easier access to visit during one's slumber in the state of sleep paralysis when the human body is most vulnerable and cannot fight back. Sleep paralysis occurs during the fourth stage of the sleep cycle, REM sleep. During sleep paralysis motor centers in the brain are inhibited although the brain is fully aware of what is happening.

Incubus and Succubus demons are responsible for what we call 'the wet dream' or nocturnal emission. In modern times such as today, some believe that these demons possess human bodies with their sex addictions causing humans to carry out their deeds, unaware, yet fully addicted. These demons pass from person to person upon sexual contact, like a spiritual sexually transmitted disease.

Some say you can pray it away, curse it away… the demons, the addictions, and the way these spirits control your life and manipulate your own manifestations.

When I heard the front door lock, I knew it was time. My cartoons played faintly in the background and I agreed to play his 'games'.

I was between 3 and 6 years old when my older half brother watched as his friends touched me in places I knew they should not have. He was my babysitter while my mom worked. He said that it didn't count because I wasn't his real sister. A real sister came from the same mother and father, according to him. And since I didn't look like him or the other siblings, he was able to disconnect this from guilt.

Love is taught by our surroundings and you learn to receive love based on the love you already know. There were 7 of them before me. 7 children existed of either my father or my mother's previous marriages. Raised by my mother, I was around her 3 the most. Ironically, her 3 teenagers were the 3 that I looked the least like. And for some reason that made them resent me even more. In some cultures, there's a silent and vocal battle between skin shades. White people tend to think racism is just a battle of one race towards another. But there are prejudices and hatred that exist inside of one's own race.
Colorism. Dark skin versus light skin. How can your siblings hate you for something you did not choose? They did. And they punished me for it.

I was the mark of their parent's divorce and while they considered me the 'pretty' child, I was a monster to them. A child doesn't know any different. It doesn't matter if people at church or the local grocery store praised the child for being "beautiful and sweet," when the child went home to be watched over by her half siblings, she... I was abused for looking different, by the people who were supposed to love me.

Sexualized by the people who were supposed to protect me.

Ostracized by people I was born adoring simply because they existed.

We don't choose our families, obviously. Unless you're among the few whom believe that before we are born, our souls choose the path and parents most able to give us the existence we feel would be most beneficial to our souls. If that is true, then yes, I could see why I chose such a fucked up family tree. Born in the midst of a sexually charged lust affair, many suffer. Mostly the child that was created if there is no love to be gained. Where do you find something that you crave when everything around you is a mirage of that desire fighting you for reasons beyond your existence?

I blocked out the memories that I no longer wanted to remember. The alternate reality kicked in. Yet, by age 9, I had already learned how to give myself an orgasm and became addicted to them.

The demon had passed on to me. And somewhere therein the connection between love and orgasms was manipulated by the demons that possessed me. If I gave them orgasms, I was told, I would be gifted with love. Incubus never left me. Incubus found his way into my dreams, my nightmares, and my reality.

CHAPTER: THE PRICE OF DEATH

They gave me a blue pill that made me feel like a super hero. I couldn't stop laughing. I felt like I was invincible. A bullet could have struck me in the middle of my eyes and I would have felt nothing. I guess that's the kind of thing they have to give you before you kill an innocent child. Luckily this was AFTER the consultation with the trained professional that the abortion clinic hired to give me a speech about my 'options' with my unborn child. I was 11 weeks pregnant and had known Anthony for only 4 months. Met him on Valentine's Day. Here it was June. I was 16. What options did I have? My mother knew I was pregnant before I did. She called him at work and threatened to have him put of the military for statutory rape. But he was well within guidelines since he was only 19. Horny idiotic teenagers, looking for love in all the wrong places. You didn't know? Dick was a place.

That morning is a morning I will never forget. It was raining violently as if it was April instead of June. $300 was the price of death. Paula Abdul's 'Rush, Rush', played on the radio as the windshield wipers foreshadowed the tears that would follow for years to come. My mother followed behind Anthony and I as we drove to the abortion clinic on a morning she had to head into work. I made a mistake. Yes. But she treated me as if I was the scum of the Earth.

I felt even more alone than I had before the events that lead me into giving this stranger my virginity in the first place. Dick was a place. Stay with me here.

As we pulled up to the abortion clinic, protestors surrounded the unmarked building. They had large pictures of unborn fetuses mutilated by the procedure of abortion. It was horrific and cruel. I did not choose to have an abortion. My mother chose for me. Yes, sure. What was I going to do with a baby? I was 16. But she didn't even bother discussing it with me. Forgiving me or counseling me through what led me to not coming to her for birth control in the first place would have been nice. I was a lonely child and became a lonely teenager searching for love. I found the closest thing to it. Anthony. Anthony's obsession with me wasn't love, but it was good enough.

So there I was, laughing hysterically in the waiting room wearing a gown, high on whatever pre-abortion medication they had given me. In hindsight, it could have been molly or MDMA. I remembered my mother's cold glare as she signed the consent form and Anthony handed over $150 dollars. I added the other half to the stack, which was my entire paycheck from my job at the Credit Union. I remembered the night I lost my virginity to this young boy whom was just as immature as I was, in my basement room while my mother slept upstairs. I remembered all the nights he had spent the night and gone unnoticed because my mother didn't notice me.

I remembered having him leave out the backdoor and asked him to ring the front door bell so that my mother could finally meet him. I remembered him asking me to marry him, placing his dog tags around my neck, and me saying, "Yes".

I laughed. I was high out of my mind. I continued to remind my Airman boyfriend how good I felt on the blue pill. Anthony sat next to me looking as if someone had already died. His face was absent of emotion. Perhaps he felt fear. Fear of my mother and her threats despite their validity. He feared that she would find a way to get him removed from the military.

"Zosia, We are ready for you," a doctor called out to me and mispronounced my name horrifically. I skipped to the chair in the dark room. They helped me place my feet into the stirrups. Anthony stood nearby and though I was still high... fear kicked in. Guilt overshadowed me. I felt the spirit of this child inside of me. But I was robbed of my choices. This child inside me was robbed of a choice. Tears fell but I did not sob. The doctor began to scrape my uterus walls with this device that felt like a vacuum sucking pieces of my own soul to be thrown into the trash bin that was emptied on Sunday afternoons into the abyss of HELL.

Another tear fell.

I bled for a few days following the abortion. Chunks of leftover fetus fell into the toilet. My mother barely spoke to me. I needed some type of counseling. I got nothing but cold shoulders. Still no family. Just the stress of my possessive relationship. His attention was misunderstood as love. His possession was misunderstood as acceptance. It was not love.
But alas, we continued to have unprotected sex. We continued to be immature children.

I broke up with Anthony a few times in the next few months. But it's really hard to give up someone whom kept promising they loved you when you have no real examples of love. They trick you into believing that this behavior is love.

 As I tell this, I must reveal that each chapter is a Zosia that has passed away, been killed, or evolved into a better one. I am a new person. My cells have been reformatted.

And, I regret NOTHING.

It was a Saturday; he held a knife to my neck for the first time. We had been together for a year. I was 17 now. Still naive. Still searching for something...

"You will never break up with me. You hear me? You're mine. I own you. I took your virginity. No one will ever own you except me," Anthony stated as we stood on a dark street near a dumpster. I envisioned my body inside of that dumpster.
"Tony. Please stop. I love you," I pleaded.

The abuse began with pinching and pushing. His playful demeanor made it hard to believe that this childlike spirit would be so cold. But apparently he was fighting his own demons. Control through abuse was the only way he knew how to fight for what he wanted. I was afraid of him but attached to his bullshit. No one knew.

Finally, I broke up with him for a week. He promised to be my friend and be a better person.

Then I took him back and to rekindle our relationship, we had sex... and he held me down, came inside of me, and whispered the following words, "Now you can never leave me." I was mortified. I knew I was pregnant. I couldn't believe after what we had went through a year prior that he would do this to me again. To himself?

My junior year was already a wreck because my mother told one of her gossip fueled friends about my abortion.
I was in HISTORY class as we discussed abortion. Inside I froze up recalling the gory details of my own procedure, but did not expect what was about to happen next.

"You know about abortion don't you, Zosia," the boy that sat in front of me said coldly with a smile. I responded with a "No," between my eyebrow furrows and felt the sting of truth in my soul.
I immediately had a flashback to that stormy June day.

I went home that evening and standing in the living room was my mother.

"Mom can I talk to you for a moment," I said placing my backpack on the steps. She wasn't very welcoming prior to my pregnancy/abortion. After the abortion, she became colder. Perhaps her own disappointments in life with her other children and their refusal to speak to her. Either way... I NEEDED my mom.

"Yes, Zosia?" my mother stated blankly with her lips tight.

"Did you tell Ann about my abortion? Because I think she told her daughter. The whole school knows and ... it's very hard to deal with right now. I thought you weren't going to tell anyone," I stated with tears in my eyes as my heart beat through my voice.

"Yes. I did," my mother said plainly without remorse. She watched the pain in my eyes and I immediately began to hate her. I hated for not being there for me before my pregnancy. I hated her for making me get an abortion. And I hated her for her lack of concern for me in this moment as I spilled my soul and wiped my tears upon the walls.

"Mom, how could you do this? It's hard enough to be a teenager. Now with this going around the school, I'm an outcast. I'm a horrible person."

"Well Zosia, you should've kept your legs closed then, huh?" My mother began walking off.

I fell to the floor in tears staring at my backpack. I wanted to run away. But where? To who? With what money? To what family? I had no one. I wasn't even sure there was a God at this point.

So back to months later...

I'm lying with my panties around my ankle as Anthony's semen began to molest the rest of my leg as the sperm that was not used slid down into sight.

Again.... How could he do this a second time? I was responsible too. But he did it on purpose. He said so. WHY? AGAIN!

For weeks, I kept asking him what we were going to do about this pregnancy. I hid it from my mother this time. I made sure I didn't give away any cues I was pregnant. She told me before that she had known I was pregnant because my eyes and hands became more regal. Some Southern old wives tale she grew up being told.

I fought to stay awake and kept my appetite hidden. She couldn't know I was pregnant a second time. I must keep it secret.

Summer came. I was about to be a senior in High School. Still pregnant. Anthony was still pretending as if the baby inside me was just going to go away. Then I felt it. I felt the child inside me kick. This baby was alive. This baby had purpose. It was ON purpose even if it was not my own.

Anthony and I were already 'Engaged', so we decided to ask my mother for consent to get married early. We planned to get me away from her, and have another abortion before spending our lives together.

He was an out for me. He was a solution to the shadows I so desperately wanted to escape.

A couple weeks before my senior year, I got information from my job at the Bank. I got the form for marriage consent. With consent in the state of Nebraska, a minor could marry at age 17.

My mother didn't think I was serious but came with me to the bank I worked at and we had her signature notarized for her consent for her 17 year old, 4th child to marry.

The following day, Anthony and I went to the courthouse and were married. We found two strangers in the Douglas County lobby to be our witnesses and I was his wife. The next day, we had $1800 to take to the abortion clinic for abortion number two. This one was harder to do. I felt the baby inside of me. I felt the soul beneath my layer of skin.

It was a sunny Saturday morning when we drove to the clinic this time. The same aborted fetus posters were outside of the clinic taunting all those that enter. This time I knew which direction not to look. I ignored their shouts. I looked up at the Sun. I looked up at God. I had been talking with him inside of myself the entire morning. Something wasn't right. My soul was heavy.

De ja vu began to ensue. I knew this day was going to be a day different than the last time I entered this place. My spirit was loud. The spirit inside me was even louder.

There I sat in the counseling session with the hired worker set to give me my 'options' prior to deciding to take the life inside of me. I DIDN'T HEAR A WORD SHE SAID. I stayed glued to the conversation with God inside of my thoughts.

"This child will be great. This child is supposed to be here," is what I kept hearing inside my spirit on repeat with a voice as profound as James Earl Jones or Morgan Freeman. Imagine the voice of God. I heard that inside of me. A voice called me to attention and made me listen. I was sitting; facing this counselor but still did not hear a word she said.

"Miss... Miss... Are you ready?" the woman asked as she stared into my face leaning towards me.

I began to smile and said, "Yes. I mean NO. No. I am keeping my baby. He will be great. I can feel him. He wants to be here. He deserves life. God wants me to keep him. I love my baby."

I screamed with joy. I felt the spirit inside me scream of relief in unison with mine.

I chose life.

CHAPTER: PUSSY KICK

There I was, curled up in a ball on the cold military housing floor, getting my pussy kicked in, just a few days after giving birth to our son. Does pussy kicking sound romantic? It wasn't. I had just walked home an hour in the snow to our duplex. Why did I walk home? This:

"I saw him looking at you, Zosia. You know that nigga," Anthony whispered clinching his teeth the way he did right before he was about to attack. "No. I promise. I swear. I don't know him," I pleaded.

Side note. I did not know him. Or any of them. But when you are married to a demon, they don't care what the truth is. Their truth is the only truth that matters. Their truth creates the reality that they live in… and they will beat you into submission.

So following the unwarranted accusations, I took my chances and walked an hour home in the freezing cold only to come home and get the tunnel that just brought human life into the world, kicked in. At one point, I felt my pussy take in his foot. I was sure it would never be the same. Every night, I thought, "I could die tonight." I ran from one situation into a fucking nightmare. Anthony, on the outside looked like a friendly guy. He was always smiling. Always making jokes.

No one knew what I was going home to. No one knew except the neighbors on the other side of the wall.

CHAPTER: PEPPERMINT HIPPO

"FUCK," I screamed. It was midnight and I sat in my Ford Focus. A chef friend of mine had just made me dinner in his restaurant. He allowed me to eat where the celebrities that came in, sat. I was treated like a Princess that night and many others since living in Las Vegas; temporarily blinding the realities that I went home to.

My car wouldn't start. It had been doing this for months. But I couldn't afford to get a new car. There were times when my account only had 25 dollars in it. My car was almost 10 years old. It worked, but not very well. I had to hold on to it for a little longer. In that moment, when my car wouldn't start, I thought of all I could call to rescue me. Not many names came to mind. The few that did were 'White girl wasted' once I did call them. In other words they were too drunk to come get me. I could call my mother.. But I didn't want to bother her even though I lived in Las Vegas as her roommate. Since a teenager, I never wanted to ask her for anything. I just wanted to forgive her and help her if I could.

But I was stranded. ..In a Las Vegas Casino Hotel parking lot. I could call my chef friend whom had just allowed all of his employees to treat me like the royalty that deep down I felt I was... but I didn't want to bother him either. I was afraid to be a burden. I felt like one my whole life.

It toughened me up to fend for myself. I had stood in food pantry lines in Nebraska for God sakes to get food for my son and myself when I lost my job(s). I filled out forms for a church to pay my rent once in Nebraska after getting fired on account of my boss whom was sexually harassing me at the time. I always found a way to survive. I could figure this out. I had to.

I began to sweat as I attempted again to start my car. I wanted to cry. But let the tears form deep in my soul. My frustration was killing me but my hope revived me. I crawled in the backseat and decided to sleep until morning. I knew my car would start by then.

The desert sunlight woke me through the tinted windows I hid behind in my slumber. I drove home towards sunrise, delighted that my car had finally started.

Her name was Renee. She was a fitness model. Rene was gorgeous. Blonde, intelligent, and addicted to Black men. She and I met on Sundays for brunch. I had dreams of being a writer. She had dreams of being rich and encouraging others to a healthy lifestyle. Sunday was cheat day for her strict diet. Sunday was my day to simply do as I loved to do; EAT. We had different ideas on money however. I saw money as necessity simply for things that mattered. Renee saw money as power. Renee loved money.
I simply wanted enough to fix my situation so that I could live comfortably and never sleep in my car again.

"I'm so tired of working at the pool. It's hot and I just can't do it anymore. This Vegas sun is no joke. UGH!" Renee stated as she looked at a menu.

"Yeah I feel you. I miss working at the pool with you once a week, but I don't think I could handle 8 hours of it for 5 days a week. That's brutal. And I'm Black enough. I'm not trying to get any Blacker," I stated with a laugh.

Renee was my blackest friend in Las Vegas even though she was White. If I wanted to know what was going on in Black pop culture or the newest Black trends, I would ask her. On the contrary, she referred to me as her White Black friend. I went with it simply because I knew my proper dialect threw people off. In America, if you happen to be brown (black) and speak eloquently, they say that you talk white without realizing how racist that statement actually is.

"So, I have this idea. I've been talking to my boo about it and he thinks I should do it," Renee says as she squeezes her lemon into her water. I already knew what she was going to say. We had joked about it when we worked modeling promotions together. I knew in this time of our own financial crunch... what she would propose. We were close. Not Best Friend close, but in Las Vegas, having anyone you could talk to openly was a blessing.

"What's your idea...," I stated raising my eyebrows while texting.

"Girls at the Peppermint Hippo make tons of money. Like 3G's a night. It's possible Zosia. You need a new car. I need a new car. All we have to do is get a business license for a couple hundred dollars. Get your Sheriff's card which means you are clear of any felonies on your record... and then audition. We're cute. They will hire us," Renee laughed.

"Seriously? I don't know Renee. I don't know if I could do that. I have an eleven-year-old child. Anything I do affects him," I said laughing but serious.

"That's exactly why you have to. You could pay off all your school debt. Focus on your writing. Focus on finally LIVING, Zosia. How else are you going to get a new car right now? You want to be somewhere in this heat stranded with your son? Who is going to save you? You must save you," Renee shrugged her shoulders as I stared out the diner window with a fork in my hand.

"Think about it. I've decided. I just think it would be easier if we both had someone to support the other while we are there," Renee stated.

A few days passed. I get a text from Renee telling me that she started working at Peppermint Hippo and was already making $2,000 a night. I started adding up the math in my head. I was barely making that much a month with the freelance modeling gigs I was doing. Yes, I was happier than I was working in an office but $2,000 a night could change my entire life. It could change my son's life. I could pay off my mother's house and help her.

We had our issues in the past but I wanted her to be happy.

I went and got my paperwork completed. I paid for my business license and my Sheriff's Card. Then on a Wednesday night, I went into Hippo to audition. Renee had made the owner aware of my presence and I was hired immediately. I had to obey protocol and put on the lingerie to walk in front of him so that he could see what my body looked like. 9 other girls did the same. It was embarrassing but necessary. It felt like a slutty line up at a brothel precinct. I saw girls with horrible bodies walk by that already were employed by Peppermint Hippo. I was intimidated nonetheless.

I was given a locker and had to fill out the forms. I had to choose a name that wasn't taken and had not been used in the past 6 months. It was so difficult not to choose a corny ass name like 'Bunny', but I wasn't a 'Bunny' type of girl. I'm a writer. I had to think of something creative. Something I could use in a story one day. (Looks at camera).
My name was 'MUSE'.

Muse. n.
1. Greek Mythology. Any of the nine daughters of Mnemosyne and Zeus, each of whom presided over a different art or science.
2. muse.
a. A guiding spirit.
b. A source of inspiration.
3. A poet

I pulled up to the backdoor, valet, and dancer entrance and awed at the parking lot. By now I had to use a screwdriver to release the brake of my car. There was this hole by the gears I placed the screwdriver in to get my car from 'Park' to 'Drive'. Embarrassing. I had to explain this to the valet driver each time I parked, smiled and handed him the screwdriver. Ashamed I was to be driving the shittiest car in view. The lot was filled with luxury cars of girls whom obviously had been successful at their dancing craft. Showing their boobs craft? Whatever. It worked. There were BMW's, BENTLEYS, MERCEDES BENZ, and JAGS.

I didn't want to do the pole dancing on stage. I wasn't quite that talented yet. Did you know it costs money to dance? If you wanted to be on stage you had to pay the door $80 a night. If you wanted to be off stage it was $130 a night. Similar to booth rent at a hair salon, I was now an independent business owner/dancer. Making the money back each night was another ball game. Private rooms and dances ranged from $200 for a half hour or $400 for an hour in VIP. I was too afraid to be seen in public doing a $20 dollar lap-dance for some guy that was going to go home to beat off in a sock to his memory of me, so I planned to make all of my money doing private dances in VIP. The catch was... what if no one wanted a dance from me? I was pretty enough or so I thought.

'Pretty' did not get the girls in there any money, however. These girls were HUSTLERS.

They said all the right things to these men to get them to spend their money. They made promises without delivering in order to gain the erection of a man and thus his wallet contents. The psychology behind the dynamic was fascinating to me.

"Girl, just think of it like being an actress. You're not lying to them. You're playing a role. They are IN here because they want that role to be played. They are in here to spend money, most of them. If that cow can get that billionaire to spend $3000 in one night... why are you sitting in this dressing room with nothing?"

Bunny was brown skinned and absolutely gorgeous. She was the type of pretty that made you want to get on your knees and beg her to leave that place. The kind of girl that Drake probably wrote his songs off of when he became famous. She said that she had worked at a bank prior and that her X husband wasn't keeping up with child support for their two children. She said it was HE that suggested she dance to make ends meet. Bunny had been there off and on for 5 years. FIVE YEARS!

Bunny made it sound so easy. I tried to take her tips of success. I just couldn't lie. I hated that. I was paying to dance and didn't make my money back some nights.

So there I was... heading to get a pizza at night. I'm on a long busy road and my car decides to cut out again at a stoplight. Frustrated, I leaned my head back in prayer and asked "God, please help me."

Just then, a 'homeless man' appeared at my window that was already rolled down. His appearance startled me as it was nighttime and I was alone. My inner monologue began to pray again and was told that this stranger was sent to help. The man in tattered clothes spoke, "I promise that I won't hurt you. I just want to help you."

So he did. He pushed my car out of traffic and another truck was behind me guiding the way so that no one hit him as he pushed me in the dark.
He pushed me about a half a mile down the street into a safe parking lot.

I offered him money. He refused. Then I gave it to him anyway and he said, "I did not help you to receive anything. I helped you because I was told to."

Told to? By who?

I didn't feel I gave him enough money, so I asked him where I could find him to repay him. He told me that wasn't necessary but if I ever needed him again... "Just look". Shortly after his sincere smile, it seemed as if he disappeared into the darkness instantly.

Every day for months, I looked for him on the same road.

I finally understand what he meant when he said "Just Look."

Hebrews 13:2: "Do not forget to entertain strangers, for by so doing some people have entertained angels without knowing it."

The next few days was spent looking for a new car while my car sat in the Wal-Mart parking lot I had a rental. I had a little bit of money saved up as well. I just felt attached to it. I didn't want to spend it on a down payment on a car and end up with car payments. But my options were limited. I had no car. I was racking up a bill with the rental car. I was driving my rental car to Hippo each night as well. At least I wasn't using a screwdriver to get my car out of park anymore, am I right?

I went to Toyota. Since I didn't have a regular 9-5 job, they wanted $10,000 down for me to have one of their brand new cars. I didn't have that. I had $5,000. Which to me was a lot of money. But despite that truth, that is ALL I had. I was getting hopeless. I still believed that I would begin to make money by showing my nipples to strangers for their entertainment and possibly a little bit of my own.

This was crunch time. I was running out of money. I took my rental car back to BUDGET rental and my mother was heading to drive me to a couple more dealerships. There was a homeless man outside of the passenger window at a stoplight. He reminded me of the man that had helped me a week prior. I had twenty dollars in my hand at the time. My spirit led me to give it to him. My mother smacked my hand and said, " You don't have a car. You need to keep your money. All of it".

"Mom, $20 dollars isn't the difference between me and another car. But it is the difference between that man and his next meal. I have food. I have shelter. I have the bare necessities. I'll be fine. I feel it," I stated and reached the $20 to him as he smiled.

That night I drove home with a new car.

They allowed me to have the car because 'Peppermint Hippo' displayed as my employer on my credit report. The dealership knew the type of money that was to be made there. I was considered 'GOOD'. I even got an extremely low interest rate. It was surreal how perfect it worked out...

Pulling up to the club valet the next day at work was met with bliss. The valet guy and I had become 'buddies' in a sense. He knew my struggle since he had parked my busted vehicle so many times. He gave me a high five as he saw that I was no longer in my Ford Focus or a golf cart sized rental.

"Nicely done. No more screw driver. Honda is a great car. And it's brand new. It's going to last you a long time, girl," he stated with a sincere smile.

"It's not a Beamer, but it runs," I said proudly.

"It doesn't need to be. These girls.. Some of them don't need those fancy cars. You'll get a fancy car one day if you want. But for now you have a reliable one. That's all that matters," he stated as he drove off in my car.

I purchased a couple cigarettes from the 'House Mom/Bathroom attendant' before heading to the floor to find someone that wanted to see my boobs at a very close range. I always thought they were great boobs. Natural but great.

In a sea of plastic Double D's when mine were real, I felt somewhat special, you could say.

Most of my time spent at Peppermint Hippo was spent admiring the gorgeous women that worked there. I wondered about their stories. Some of which were actually shared with me. A couple women were teachers with double lives who lived in nearby states. Others were real estate agents. One was even a nurse with a lot of college debt. Sitting or standing in the darkness, I was like an undercover spy, unintentionally eavesdropping on conversations as I hoped someone would ask me to dance.

On my last day at Peppermint Hippo, I decided to break a couple rules. I went on stage when I was not supposed to. I made accidental eye contact with a famous R&B singer whom happened to be in attendance that evening. He was staring at me intently. I never really gave much of a shit about a celebrity. Good people with good hearts excite me. But as advised by one of the other girls, "black male entertainers are the biggest tricks. Especially the rappers. If you see one, feed his ego and flashy image. They're the ones that love strippers the most. It's a status symbol for them."

Anyway, He along with a female pop singer were both sitting together.

He asked me to come to him. I showed no emotion although my inner monologue was excited for the chance to see him up close and discover if he was a nice person or not. NOPE. Another entertainer joined him. There was an awards show going on in Las Vegas that night, and Hippo was the place they chose to come afterward.

The female pop singer asked that I get on stage. So for the experience, I decided to attempt at stage dancing for her. I failed hilariously.

"Gul' you too scary. Get off da' stage gul'. You don't know how to pop yo' pussy right," the female pop singer stated in her thick island accent.

I decided to turn it up a notch as the pop singer's song came on. She started clapping, screaming, and throwing bills at me. I was feeling myself until my nervous, sweaty palms caused me to slip right off of the pole.

I laughed because at the same moment security came to get me because I was not supposed to be on stage that night. I cut someone else's turn short because I knew it was going to be my last night there anyway. I grabbed my bra and a couple of dollars and smirked as I exited the stage. That same night, Renee had been called to VIP as she always was. VIP girls made 400 each hour. The owner Joe liked Renee and was rumored not to like Black people unless they were rich and coming in there to buy his girls and thus put money in his pocket. I stood next to Renee talking to her as she stood by VIP awaiting the 'Important People'.

I hardly go to talk to Renee anymore.

"Are you having fun?" Renee asked. "Yeah. I guess. It's definitely a life experience I did not expect to have. How are you doing," I asked adjusting my bra and fanning smoke away. "I'm great girl. I made 3 G's last night. BALLIN'," Renee joked as I admired her perfectly toned body and platinum blonde hair. She was definitely a go-getter. Just then, Joe came up to us and saw me standing with Renee. Angry to see me near VIP when I wasn't called, he shoos me away and says "Get away from here" as if this was 1941, before the Civil Rights Movement, and I was too close to his property. I felt bad. I knew he didn't like Black people but thought I had a temporary pass by being friends with his favorite worker. Reality kicked in. I was still BLACK.

Only few dances were had on my 8-day stint at the Peppermint Hippo. I had to stretch my employment days out because I was spending my savings simply to show up for work. It was expensive. I was NOT making $2000 a night as Renee was. I began to see that I wasn't supposed to be there. It was an experience. Psychology research if you will... and a front row seat to some of the most beautiful naked women you have ever seen in your fucking life. Dressing room privileges were grand. Naked girls giggling, lotion application, and EVERYTHING you can imagine...

CHAPTER: GUILTY BY ASSOCIATION

She stood there glowing in the light. Naked. Her brown skin glistened as if the sun grew lips, put on Chanel lip-gloss and kiss her itself. I sat on her bed facing the bedroom bathroom where she stood with her perfectly manicured toes femininely caressing the tiles. Lynn looked over her shoulder and smiled at me as if I were a man, with eyes that begged me to take off my clothes and join her in the shower.

I looked across the room at the wig she had taken off earlier, revealing her short curly hair beneath. Lynn was gorgeous with and without the wig. Her frame was small but she was dominant. I was submissive even though I was larger than her in size. Her supple breasts were enough to fit my long fingers across in a perfect cupping. Mine were a hand full that only Andre the Giant could handle. I removed my clothing as she waited for me anxiously. I fumbled awkwardly as I attempted to unhook my own bra that I had unhooked many times for many years prior to this. You could say I was nervous. I was in an unfamiliar town in an unfamiliar state; with a woman I met online years ago. I met her through a modeling website. She had lost her mother at a young age and admired that I was a single mother. I booked a photo shoot in Dallas with a photographer that she knew and we scheduled time to meet.

Earlier that day:

My shoot had just ended. I heard the door open to the studio and knew it was her coming in to pick me up. Daniel the photographer was excited for me to meet her as well. Lynn entered and gave me a stare that I was not expecting. I was older than she was, but felt shy for some reason. There were still many experiences I had not had and some of them made me skittish.

"You're even prettier in person," Lynn said pulling her eyeglasses down as I blushed. She made one of those grunting noises of satisfaction as she came closer. We then hugged like old friends whom went a while without seeing one another. "Want to get something to eat, " Lynn asked as she bit her tongue and looked at me as if I were on the menu.

Naive, I pretended she was just being playful. She was too pretty to like girls, I thought...

I thought girls that liked girls were supposed to appear butch like, manly. Not feminine and soft. Those types of lesbians were only on Cinemax.

Visiting from Nebraska, people were always fascinated with my location and whether or not Black people lived there.

Lynn loaded my things in her truck and took me to meet John, her boyfriend.
"So you're a photographer in Los Angeles Lynn tells me? That's cool that you travel from Dallas to LA frequently," I said in the backseat facing John.

Lynn was driving but looked in the rearview and gave me a scowl as if I said something wrong. I knew instantly something was off but I wasn't sure. "Huh," John asked unsure if he heard me correctly himself. Lynn's scowl fades and she says, "Sorry baby, Zosia is confused, I was telling her that I did a shoot in LA and was taking her to meet you. She must have got the conversations mixed up."

Sitting in the bedroom with Lynn's boyfriend we discussed religion, Nebraska, and sexuality. John was a hardcore Christian with no tolerance for any type of same gender love or sexuality. His views were so strong that I didn't want to argue so I stayed quiet. I also stayed quiet because I was sure that his girlfriend had a crush on me.

Having an affinity for the misfits of society gave me a different outlook. The gays, the lesbians, the transgendered, and the misunderstood. I was a misfit myself after all. The only people I could not tolerate are those that hated others. And John was THAT guy. He began to bash the LGBT community so hard that I got really uncomfortable and decided to tune him and his charming southern accent OUT. Such a shame for such a handsome face and accent to go to waste. I wondered why Lynn was with him.

...So there I was, awkwardly removing my bra in Lynn's bedroom as she watched awaiting me to join her. She began to walk towards the shower. By now she knew my destination was her. I had to make this memory as hot as possible without tripping over my own panties.

46

Immediately upon opening the shower door, the steam reached my skin and took my breath away. My breath was replaced with hers as she kissed me softly, the way that only a woman could kiss another woman. It was sensual and innocent. She began to caress me with her sponge and washed me thoroughly yet gently.

While washing me, I looked around, admiring the balcony view overlooking the city of Dallas and the skyline. She carried me to her bed and had her way with me. 4 inches shorter than me, she overpowered anything that I could protest. She was like a naked magic pixie fairy.

Lynn threw me upon her bed. The satin comforter opened its legs for my entrance as I landed and bounced. Lynn immediately crawled on top of me. She opened my legs and began to kiss me in places I didn't realize were sensitive because they had never been explored the way that they were right then. She opened her drawer and in it were an abundance of toys. I knew she frequented this drawer as the location of each device within the drawer was memorized by her hand.

I don't like toys but allowed her to do as she wished so that I could live in this moment with her. Panting and kissing one another with femininity combined. The phone rang. It was John. We had to be at the restaurant in the next hour to meet John on time. Lynn had other plans...

"Here. Put this on," Lynn placed out her own clothing for me to wear. She did my hair and my make up as if I was her personal Barbie doll sex toy for the evening. I went with it. It was kind of cool to be catered to by a woman or anyone for that matter. I wasn't used to being treated this way. I liked it. A LOT. At her request, there were no panties worn this evening.

We hopped in her truck and headed to a restaurant in the city. This part of Dallas had something that I was not used to seeing in such abundance; White men with Black women. I knew it existed. My mother's former fiancé' was a white man. It was just so abundant there; I didn't know where I was. I was fascinated by the acceptance and abundance. In Nebraska, there were plenty of Black male/(other) inter-racial couples but most White men were afraid to make a pass at me even if I looked interested in return.

The restaurant was extremely fancy even for my taste at the time. I was 25 and had not seen many fancy places in Nebraska like this.

We entered the restaurant holding hands as if we were a newly engaged lesbian couple. Uncomfortable at the stares, I decided to ignore for her beautiful grace that I endured with confidence as we walked towards a tall white gentleman whom I guessed was Lynn's 'meeting'.

"Who's your friend Lynn," the gentleman asked reaching for my hand as he led us to a table with a panoramic view of the nightlife outside. "This is Zosia, Jeff. Isn't she adorable," Lynn said squeezing my hand then clenching her eyes. I blushed and introduced myself to the stranger.

"You two seem awfully fond of one another. How did you meet," Jeff asked observing the sensual behavior and erotic chemistry taking place between my lover and I. "Well, she is a writer. A friend of mine bought one of her books online. And she came to town to model for a photographer I have worked with," Lynn replied softly. I was perturbed that Jeff thought I was a lesbian. I was not. I was simply wrapped up in a moment and enjoying the affections of a beautiful woman who frequently reminded me how incredible she thought I was.

Lynn and I sat beside one another across the table from Jeff. At one point, Jeff handed Lynn a white envelope. I imagined the possibilities of what was in the envelope. Still unsure who this man was to her, I let my mind wander. It had come to my attention that she had a lot of male suitors. None of which John knew of.

We ordered dinner and barely finished when her phone rang. I saw her boyfriend John's name light up the caller ID on her cell phone. Anxiety kicked in as she whispered without fear, "John's here. I'm going to meet him at the restaurant next door. You excuse yourself and follow in five minutes."

My first thought? Is this bitch crazy? Did she know John was coming this whole time? Why are we sitting with Jeff? Why was she holding my hand and treating me like her own living breathing Cabbage Patch doll? And more importantly, we're about to meet homophobic John, and I still don't have any panties on at her request.

"I need to freshen up in the little girl's room, darling. I'll be right back," Lynn faced Jeff's blue eyes, as she appeared to be going to the restroom. Nervously, each minute felt like an hour as I was left in this bourgeois restaurant with this tall stranger. "Soooo... you um, do you like living in Dallas," I asked looking at the large clock over our table. Small talk. "I love Dallas. I'm in computer programming. I make a lot of money and travel a lot. Lynn is supposed to go to Tahiti with me next month. You should join us. Do you like the beach," Jeff asked, touching my hand with his finger as I slowly pulled away.

Awkward laughter followed as I choked on my water. "I'm going to check on Lynn. I'll. Be. Right. Back," I whispered wanting thank him for the meal, but not able to admit that I wouldn't be back because the woman I had just let go down on me was a trifling piece of work and my ride back to my hotel. My heartbeat became louder each step I got to the exit. I considered calling a taxi to take me clear across town but my suitcase was at her house!

"Keep walking Zosia. Don't look back. Jeff won't notice. Sneak to the exit. Look like you're going to the bathroom," I was having an inner monologue and making myself laugh somehow at getting into such a predicament. Outside of the restaurant couples held hands, walked the town, and smiled. It was one of the most beautiful nights I have seen.

Lynn's hand appeared in the midst of an outside patio ahead, waving me over to her and John, her stiff boyfriend.

"Hey girl. Where you been," Lynn asked me as if I was the one that just flaked on a nice guy in a restaurant. Who plans two dates the same night in the same area? LYNN. Was I date number 3? Never mind that. I sat down at the table. This time I was in Jeff's position as Lynn cuddled next to her boyfriend John and we began to make small talk from across the table.

About 20 minutes went by and Jeff appeared outside of our patio seating, shaking his head at Lynn and smiling. He didn't necessarily look mad.
But I couldn't bare make eye contact with him, even if it wasn't my fault. I was guilty by association.

"I just think two men together is absolutely disgusting. How can anyone not want a woman? Women are beautiful, delicate, and fascinating. It's unholy for two men to rub dicks anyway," John rambled doing his usual prejudice speech on how straight people are better than gay people. My stomach began to turn because I grew to despise him and his voice. During his speech, Lynn slid her sandal off and placed her toes in between my pantie-less legs. In that moment, I didn't know how to feel. I felt like John would brutally beat me if he knew that his girlfriend and I had slept together a couple hours ago. I felt like 'the other man' yet so much woman at the same time. I was fragile, aroused by her toe in my vagina, and vulnerable from situations I had going on at home in Nebraska.

"What do you think about that, Zosia," Lynn asked with a serious face while her toe was planted inside of me underneath the table. "What do I think about what," I responded. I assume I had a look of terror on my face because I finally realized she was nuts and wanted me to give my opinion on her boyfriend's strong beliefs, while she dug for my splashes to occur.

I thought she was taking me back to my hotel that evening but she insisted that she was too tired once we got to her place.

She said she would take me in the morning. John spent the night that night. He lay in my wet spot on her bed. I slept on the couch directly outside of the double doors that led to her bedroom and listened to the two of them moan for hours. Each time I attempted to turn the television louder, she took it as a challenge and proceeded to scream of bliss. I couldn't tell if she was just a psychotic bitch who loved a show or if she genuinely wanted me to be jealous. Either way after taking me to my hotel the next day, I never saw her again... until she sent me a friend request on Facebook years later.

CHAPTER: CHOPPED AND SCREWED

A napkin full of cum is one of the most disgusting things to find on your desk. I picked it up and sniffed it while dissecting the snot like substance on the decorated paper towel full of stars and shapes. The slime looked fresh. I knew he was in here masturbating to his favorite porn fetish again: 'Young black men and older white women'. If it wasn't that one, it was the BIG BLACK ASS on the BangBros website.

In recent decades porn went from something your undersexed middle-aged father resorted to by means of a hidden Playboy magazine that he pulled out when no one was home. But this man was not undersexed. He had a young, willing woman who was in love with him and willing to succumb to any fantasy that he may have had. But the realization that I still wasn't enough made the stomach acid rise to my lips as I crumbled the napkin in my hands. I began to recall the countless women he told me were just friends and their likeness to his porn fetishes.

When we started dating, he pretended to go to work every day at a job he never had, living in his parent's guesthouse until I decided to take him in. What began as just my boyfriend sleeping over ended up being a man living with me rent-free. Taking care of a grown man that has no aspirations of his own but to roller-skate became a burden.

"Seriously? You still can't get wet? What the fuck is the matter with you," Scooter scolded as he lay in my bed. I couldn't believe 13 years after meeting Scooter, whom was my first love, that he had become such a self serving shit head. I sent him roses when I was 15. Would have chosen him over any and everything. But there I was at 27, sitting in my bed at 7 a.m. with tears in my eyes because my vagina had finally rejected the man that never deserved me. The man that convinced me and others of so many lies. The Prince Charming of Bull Shit.

Scooter was always into something and very passionate about whatever hobby he decided to take up. At the time of my graduation, he was 20 and had just got into a motorcycle accident. Flashback to then, I was 23, Scooter was 25, and I ran into him at a function on a night I didn't plan to go anywhere with a female cousin I had just learned about. Her and I met in the bathroom of a modeling competition.

"You're so pretty," I stated into the sandalwood toned girl's mirror reflection as she combed her hair. "Aww, thank you, sweetie. You're very pretty too," she responded. I stared at her longer hoping she wasn't alarmed by my curiosity. There was something familiar about her that I couldn't quite place my finger on, so I tested it. "You look like one of my sisters. One of my father's daughters," I said looking at how bright and wide her eyes were.

"Oh really," she laughed, "what is your sister's name?" "Simone Vaugeois," I responded, sure that she wouldn't know who that was.

"That's my cousin's name," she exclaimed. "Really, that's crazy? What are your other cousin's names," I questioned feeling as if I stepped into the twilight zone as other women in the bathroom eavesdropped on our conversation in disbelief. After some research, we found out that our father's were first cousins and their mothers were sisters. Lisa and I had just discovered we were cousins. I was excited, embarrassed, and slightly furious when she told me about a family reunion which had occurred recently. My father attended, yet somehow 'forgot' to invite me. Guess you would think I was used to it by age 23. But I wasn't. Lisa and I began to talk on the phone and she invited me to go out with her to a nightclub. I had a 5-year-old child at the time and was never much into the nightlife scene. When I wanted that stage of life, I didn't have a sitter, so I just got used to being at home.

Lisa and I met in West Omaha for a Networking party at a nightclub called 'Nico'. Shortly into the night, I spotted my high-school sweetheart Scooter. I heard two voices in my head the moment I saw him. The first voice said, "Keep walking Zosia. Don't turn around. Keep going. He didn't want you at 15, 16, 19, and won't be any different at 23."

The second voice was clearly temptation and somehow said less but managed to win, 'Turn around." And so I did. I turned around.

Scooter and I began talking and he was enamored with adult Zosia. It was flattering. I was a grown woman now. I wasn't a kid anymore.

I could do things.. Like have sex with him if I wanted to. Did I want to?

Somehow we ended up racing home to his place once the club closed at 1am. He lived in a small house next door to his parents that he said he purchased when his last X and he split. How convenient. That night began the 4-year relationship that ended a few months before I moved to Vegas and promised his mother not to answer his calls.

So since High School, Scooter was still passionate about his motorcycle but had taken up a new hobby and done so quite well. He was now a Jam Roller Skater. I hadn't roller-skated since grade school. I was almost 24 years old and had no idea how to balance on 8 wheels. But they say 'Love is Insanity'. And quite frankly, insane people try anything. He never knew it back then but God could have placed any other human in the world in the same room with me and the only person I would see was 'Scooter'. I took up Roller-skating so that I could fit into his world. I left my own world behind. But what world was that?

I was struggling to fit in to a world that I deemed cruel for a single Black mother raising a son with a dream and no college education.

Scooter was the popular grown up kid at the roller-skating rink. When he first took me to the rink, other girls laughed at me. His former flings, fucks, and those whom wished for a ride ... on his dick or with his skates. I didn't care. He initially seemed to only have eyes for me.

I began skating by holding the wall as if I was back in kindergarten again. I was also in those funky brown rentals that everyone's feet had been in. Eventually I graduated and purchased Speed Skates. Jam skaters know that those are not 'Gliding' skates. Gliding means to roll more gracefully on the rink and with your moves. I wanted to be cool. I wanted to be smooth. I wanted to roll like they roll in Chicago, Memphis, Houston, Little Rock, and St. Louis. I tried. I got pretty good for someone with a neurological tremor and natural clumsiness. But still, I was not good enough.

"Zosia, you can't come to Chicago anymore with me. Or any other trip for that matter. You're not as good as the other girls and it's starting to embarrass me," Scooter stated as we sat in my living room.
"But, I've been trying. I'm doing my best. Those girls have been skating much longer than I have. I just started when I re-met you," I whispered holding back tears that connected to previous conversations and problems that had arisen from girls, Scooter, and the roller skating rink.
I let Scooter move in with me shortly after we got together. The house that he said he purchased, it turns out was his parent's guest house that he was in after getting put out from his X's home. 6 months into the relationship, every kiss was a band-aid over a lie. Every fuck was him using my pussy to imagine someone else's. Someone with the bigger ass that he once said he wished that I had.

Of course I didn't realize this until I came home one day to find the internet window opened up to his latest sex fetish and a napkin on my desktop full of his semen. The rejection in those moments was deep. He began having sex with the computer while I still lusted after this man that clearly did not want me. As a very young girl I thought that if I really loved a man and did everything he wanted, acted out his every fantasy because I wanted to, allowed him to cum wherever he please and imitated the scenes I saw in the porn I found in his internet history... I thought this was going to make him love me. I thought one day I could be enough.

Scooter began stomping his feet and crying the day I broke up with him for the first time after finding the napkin and him lying and saying it wasn't his. It startled me that he could lie so easily about something so evident belonged to no one but him. It was the first time I had the strength to leave him. His tears that day made me sympathize with him. His words were, "I'm not ready for this to be over." He stomped like a 2 year old having a tantrum.
I never feared Scooter or anything. He wasn't that kind of guy. He was just an idiot looking for a girlfriend that would allow him to do whatever he wanted to do. I was her this time. It was someone else before me and would be someone else one day.

I really did like roller-skating. I wanted to get good at it. I wanted to be as good as the other girls. Tears started rolling as I realized all I had been allowing Scooter to put me through. He wasn't paying his portion of the rent so that he could go on these skate trips. And the skate trips were amazing. I understood his awe. It was 500-2000 people together passionately skating shoulder to shoulder, doing tricks, dancing, and loving one another all for the sake of music and art.

Scooter was the 'ring leader' of those at the Bellevue Skating rink known as Skate City. Everyone looked to him for the decision making and planning of the days to carpool and ride to join the rollers in Kansas City for their Sunday Soul Night of Adult Skating. Nebraska's events never had that many good skaters. Out of 200 people at the skate nights in Nebraska, 15 were good skaters and the rest were spectators. That's not a good ratio at all. In other cities like Chicago, KC, Memphis, and ATL, the ratio was the opposite. EVERYONE could skate and if you couldn't skate you got ran over, scolded to learn how to skate, or escorted off the rink by someone who feared for your life.

Jam Skating was magical. The sweating and the energy that rolled passed you along with the smiles on everyone's faces. There were no fights just love. There was a lot of 'sharing' however. Lots of drama in the roller-skating world. It was like a mini soap opera featuring all kinds of people. A Japanese roller from Japan used to come every year to the Chicago roll every July. Yes, Japanese. AND he COULD ROLL!

"Scooter. I just can't get wet. Since we broke up you only come over to have sex with me.

My body knows it and doesn't like it anymore. I need love," I said as tears fell with a thud upon my naked legs. "Whatever Zosia. There you go with that poetic BULL SHIT. Miss me with that. I'm Scooter. You know me already. Let another nigga come over here and romance you. You've known me for 13 years and we were together for 4 of them. We don't need foreplay anymore," Scooter said coldly. I began to cry harder, feeling sorry for myself and angry that I could love someone who clearly didn't give a shit about me. I couldn't understand how he could be so cruel. "But Scooter, I want more than sex. I know we technically aren't together anymore but I don't want to be just sex," I cried.

"Be happy I'm coming to you for sex and not someone else. You should feel privileged," Scooter said.

"Privileged," I repeated inside myself.

I began to cry harder with every word he spoke. I was his whore. I was once forced to wear a fake engagement ring and now reduced to THIS. "What? The other girls I see don't get to fuck me. That's all you. And you're clean. I don't have to wear a condom with you," Scooter said still sitting in my bed. My mouth could hardly form any more words to say because I was in disbelief that I was simply a clean vagina to fuck. The pain I felt in that moment is a pain I still have not felt since that day.

I stood up to the bathroom in my room and began wiping my nose. "Scooter, I can't do this anymore. We cannot keep doing this anymore. This has to end right now," I said quietly between tears. "Zosia, Please, you always say that. 'Scooter, we can't do this anymore, blah blah bull shit. Miss me with that. You're not going anywhere," Scooter said mocking me by cartooning his voice.

"Yes, I do always say that. And I always mean it. We can't. I don't call you or bother you after I say it. I don't contact you AT ALL once I say it. I stay away," I cried while snot ran down my face.

Scooter still laying on my bed in the dark as the sun shined through my blinds then said the statement that changed my heart forever, "Yeah, you're right. YOU don't call me. You don't bother me when you say you're done. BUT you forgot one thing. YOU ALWAYS ANSWER WHEN I CALL YOU."

In an instant something came over me as if I was awakened from the dead. My tears dried, my snot stopped rolling as if my nose was immediately stuffed up, and my neck tilted to the side like I was possessed with an idea from an outer force. That's when I said, "GET OUT." I didn't see him again after walking him to the garage to retrieve his car. He repeatedly kept reminding me that I would be back and I didn't mean it. He was wrong. So very wrong. I appreciate him waking me up from the nightmare I had been living for 4 years with him, my so-called 'Dream Lover'. NOT. When I woke up I was disgusted by my entire relationship with him. At one point his dick was inside of me. I ALLOWED that. I allowed the semen of a monster to splash upon my organs.

———

A couple weeks after telling Scooter goodbye, his phone calls continued. I did NOT answer. I did however have a dream one night about being invited to a Women's Conference at a church. When I woke the next day, I had an email invite from a girl I barely knew to the church that Scooter's mother attended. I adored his mother. She was so kind, gentle, honest, and motherly.

I wished so many times she had been my mother. His family was so Cosby show perfect other than him. Subconsciously I know why I stayed with him.

Anyway, where were we? Ah, the Women's Conference invitation. After having a dream about it, I knew I had to go when I was invited the next day. My dreams had this interesting way of guiding me on certain occasions. I definitely felt this was one of those times. The Women's Conference was a 3-day event. On the final day of the event, I saw Mrs. Andrews, Scooter's lovely mother whom I loved as my own. The women were having breakfast in the cafeteria of the church preparing for the guest speaker Vivian Rogers of Dallas.

"So how have you been? I've missed you. So has Mr. Andrews. We miss little man too. You'll have to bring him by for Easter," Mrs. Andrews said holding my hand beneath the table as we ate. "Been good. Better. Getting my life together. Thinking about starting school soon. I've been trying and think this time it will finally work. Also been talking to my mother. Thinking about moving there to get away from here and closer to California," I said with a small smile. "REALLY? Honey I just think that is fantastic. I have always seen great things for you. You have to see it for yourself though. It won't happen if you don't believe," Mrs. Andrews squealed with an assured faith.

"I know, I've just been. I've been dealing with a lot. I'm trying to get my life together. It's hard. I want a family. I want a career. I really miss you guys. But I don't want to disrespect Scooter and keep in contact with you against his wishes. He despised when his other exes did it, so I don't want to do it and get under his skin. I haven't seen him in 2 weeks now," I stated as tears began to fall again. It was getting embarrassing because I now was balling. I really loved Scooter. "Scooter says he hasn't seen you since November. It's been a while huh," Mrs. Andrews stated. That's when I really began to cry because he was lying to his mother about me. It was March and I had just seen him two weeks prior. I explained to Mrs. Andrews the exchange that had taken place and she made me pinky promise to never answer his calls again. She loved her son but agreed that he was not good for me. She was disappointed in him for treating me that way and me for allowing it.

Vivian Rogers was a great pastor. She began her portion of the Women's Conference with a lot of profound statements about God and his vision on our lives. Then she approached the end of her sermon and said this, "There's a woman in here right now who is going through something that God is going to use to benefit her one day. This woman has a gift and easily relates to other women. You're a writer.

You will share your story one day and heal many others. You will heal women. You will heal men. You will use what you are going through.

Do not be afraid. You are also on the verge of a move. Move. Go. You know what you are supposed to do. God put a vision and a purpose on your life. He gave you a gift. In the name of Jesus I want you to bow your head with me and pray and receive this blessing. Do you agree with me?"

Vivian and the entire congregation were looking directly at me. It was as if someone told her my story but no one had the time to do so that quickly. I had pastors attempt a prophecy over me in the past. All of them were wrong. It made me uncomfortable when they were wrong in the past. Made me think that religion was phony and these fake prophecies were given like gypsies telling a fortune in attempt to get money. Vivian however, she was spot on in areas that I had only talked about with God. Tears began to flow and I wasn't even embarrassed of the camera that was recording the Women's Conference, Vivian, and my tears of revelation.

I avoided the roller-skating rink on the nights I knew Scooter would be there. I couldn't bear seeing him again. Not that I was ashamed, I was afraid that I might find a brick and throw it at his face. I wrote the BEST poetry during that break up.

I finally got so sick of avoiding the places he may be that I moved to Las Vegas. Depending on perspective, Las Vegas is the best or worst place to go following a heartbreak.

CHAPTER: BLACK BUNNY

"Stop playing with your boobs," Charlene laughed. Charlene and I moved to Las Vegas around the same time for different reasons. "I'm really happy you invited me. Are my boobs okay? It feels so strange walking around in heels at a pool," I stated admiring the scenery adorned with beautiful palm trees, people, and cabanas. My feet were killing me. I didn't go to the pool in Nebraska. Though I always wanted to learn, I couldn't swim. Typical Black stereotype, right? Vegas pools didn't require swimming however. In Las Vegas, people went to the pools to be seen, socialize, and get so sloppy drunk that they were peeing in the pool while making out with strangers.

I was there to make friends. I had just quit my first Vegas job as a Hotel Front Desk clerk to spend more time with my son who I felt I was away from far too much by being gone 10 hours a day to a job that was not conductive to who I wanted to be.

A month before this pool outing, I met Renee at an audition who convinced me that I could model full time, make more money, and be happier. It sounded like a great idea. The moment I met Renee she had a knack for making me believe I could do anything. *Cough* Peppermint Hippo flashback.

I quit my front desk clerk job a week after meeting Renee and as expected I had more time to focus on my son, school, and my dream.

I've always had this theory about Las Vegas before moving there. My theory was that at some point everyone comes to Las Vegas for some reason or another. Some come for business meetings as Las Vegas is filled with Convention Centers. Some come for pleasure. Las Vegas advertises freedom from reality in the overused campaign "What Happens in Vegas, Stays in Vegas". Others come for a fresh start in a town where you can be anything...

So there I was, walking the pool with Charlene and her boring friend. I had to stop every few minutes to massage my feet because let's face it, I wasn't the kind of girl to wear heels that much. Adjusting to the Las Vegas glamour scene was met with a hilarious challenge. The challenge of me learning to be 'Beautiful' instead of just 'Interesting'. The challenge of figuring out how to balance in heels while splashing in water every few feet without falling into the pool. And most importantly, how not to let Las Vegas change me.

The wind could have accompanied us on this day as it was so far the hottest day I had experienced since moving to Las Vegas. Always a fan of a slushed alcoholic beverage, I focused on the beautiful day and the fact that "I live in Las Vegas!"

"Mind if we find a seat somewhere? I saw Jorge, this guy I know at a cabana on the other side of the pool. Told him I would come by and say hi later. I'm sure he wouldn't mind if we sat for a few and rest our feet," I said watching the tourists and locals splash water as the DJ spun B.O.B. & Bruno Mars' song 'Nothing on You'.

We approached the cabana on the opposite end of the pool. It was crowded with servers. I did not see Jorge. I did see a handsome middle-aged man with his shirt off wearing pool shorts. "Can I help you, gorgeous," the man asked staring at me with concern. "Hello. I'm looking for Jorge. He was here earlier and said I could come back to sit for a bit," I said trying to talk over the loud crowd. "You're welcome to stay as long as you like, gorgeous," the gentleman stated as he showed his way inside of the cabana, which now appeared to be his purchase.

Charlene and I followed the mysterious stranger into the shaded cabana as the fan blew over our heads. "Who is he," Charlene inquired. "I don't know. I don't care. He's nice and he's letting us sit down," I whispered between my teeth smiling at the servers whom appeared to be waiting for their next instruction.

"Please. Please. Have a seat. Your friend too," the handsome stranger insisted using a towel to wipe the excess sweat from his chest. I sat close enough to hear him if he spoke but far enough to make sure he knew I was just there to sit. Besides, I was still getting over my Australian affair. I didn't want to send any mixed messages to this man.

"What's your name, gorgeous," the handsome man asked. "Zosia. It's like Sasha but with a Z," I laughed at my own corniness. Handsome man seemed to think it was charming. He blushed and moved an inch closer.

"My name is Vincent. Or Vince. Whichever you prefer, gorgeous," handsome man smiled at me.

"So what do you do? How long have you been in Las Vegas," Vince asked as I prepared to ramble on like the fresh Las Vegas meat I was. "Well, I'm from Nebraska. I moved here to be closer to California a few months ago. I just quit my front desk job at one of the hotels here. All the typing made it tiring to do my schoolwork when I get home. I'm also a student. I study psychology. And I'm a writer. Hoping the move here will open some doors for me in the writing realm also," I rambled as Charlene played with the text messages on her phone. "You sound like you have a really good head on your shoulders, gorgeous. Zosia. You definitely have a beautiful head on your shoulders," Vincent stated.

"Can I get you anything," Vincent began.

"Hey, bring her and her friend whatever she wants. Champagne, Vodka, Slushies, whatever she wants. Hear?," Vincent stated towards the workers who immediately ran off to gather his requests.

"Actually, I'm okay. Water is fine. Thank you. I appreciate that," I replied feeling overwhelmed and sorry for the workers who seemed stressed. It was such a pretentious question to ask, but I didn't want to be rude since he asked me first. I slowly asked, "So what do you do in Las Vegas? You like it here?"

"I own a large percentage of various successful properties here in town," Vincent responded without blinking an eye or seeming as if it was a big deal at all. "Oh. Cool," I responded realizing the actions of those around us were a reflection of what he just said. Charlene scooted closer when she heard what he said, almost pushing me to move closer to him. I wasn't interested in his money. I wanted my own. But he was handsome. THAT was interesting. And my Aussie lover had disappointed me thoroughly. One his penis was the size of my pinky finger and two; he was still in love with his heroin addict X who lived in Tokyo. So, hey.. why not flirt with handsome older man, I mean... Vincent.

Charlene and I had a couple of drinks in the cabana de Vincent. He was really nice and extremely charming. I liked his nickname for me, 'Gorgeous'. I couldn't decide if that was because he couldn't remember Zosia or simply thought I was.
Either way, surrounded by a sea of plastic breasts and fake lips, I appreciated him appreciating me.

In Nebraska, men outside of my own race were hesitant to hit on me. In Las Vegas, they had no fear. AWESOME. "What are you doing tomorrow, gorgeous," handsome man asked. I looked at Charlene as if I needed her approval to make a decision. After hiding behind the front desk for my first six months in Las Vegas, I didn't know about new men. I met my Aussie lover WHILE behind the front desk. He was checking out. I liked meeting people in 'safe circumstances' where I could run a background check if necessary.

Regardless of Vincent owning some property in the town I currently rested my ass cheeks upon, he was new. I had no referrals. He could very easily be a rich man looking for a girl to tie up in his mansion and make a sex slave out of. My imagination got carried away.

"Zosia, what are you doing tomorrow? Would you like to have lunch or dinner with me? Or both," Vincent said regaining my attention after my inner monologue moment with myself. "Oh, I'm sorry. Yes. I have to work a modeling promotion tomorrow at another pool but maybe after," I said while contemplating how I would finish my homework, work, and have time for a date with handsome man.

"What time are you finished with work?"

"I am done at 3pm. I can come after," I said.
"I'll have my assistant call you at 3pm with instructions."

"Okay. See you tomorrow then. Nice meeting you."

"Nice meeting you too, gorgeous," handsome man stated, grabbing his towel and exiting the cabana.

The next day I had a modeling gig at another pool and was eagerly watching the clock for 3pm. I was also nervous that I would be wet with sweat by the time I arrived my date with Vincent. Hadn't had many dates in Las Vegas. Would have preferred the opportunity to go home and shower prior to meeting with him but he insisted that I come as I was directly after work. And so I did.

At 3pm sharp, Vincent's assistant called me and gave me the instructions on where to meet him. I followed the directions given by the audio map on my phone. A half hour later, I arrived a private airport and stared into the town surrounded with majestic mountains.

I began to get uneasy wondering why we were at an airport for lunch. Envisioning what lie ahead, and feeling the heat from the desert sun upon my skin as I rolled down my car window and was greeted by his assistant, a bubbly male who had a warm smile.

"Zosia," the cheeky male asked as I politely responded.
"Yes, I am Zosia," I said getting out of my car and turning on the alarm.

"Do you have everything you need," he asked.

"Um. I think so."

"I'm sorry. I'm Charles. Vincent's assistant of 11 years. You were probably 11 when I started working for him," Charles spoke with a means to compliment on my youthful look. Charles reached for my hand and shook it eagerly as if he was being watched.

"Nice to meet you Charles," I smiled, "where are we headed?"

"There's a slight change of plans. I hope you don't mind.

Vincent had to catch a flight out this morning and is at his residence in LA which is a 30-40 minute flight away depending on the pilot," Charles laughed.

"Oh. LA? Right now? He wants me to fly to LA to have lunch with him? Buut…" I began as Charles interrupted.

"Don't worry. Sasha.. is it," Charles interrupted ending with a question.

"Zosia."

"My apologies. Don't worry Zosia. Our pilot Fred will bring you back to Las Vegas whenever you are ready. Again it's only a short ride back home. Vince is very excited to see you," Charles reassured me with a nudge.

I didn't think about it too long. I spent most of my life living in perpetual fear of strangers and their intentions because of "Stranger Danger" and seeing one too many episodes of CSI.

"Ok. I'll go," I smiled as Charles grabbed my backpack full of things I didn't leave the house without.

Charles led me to the stairs of the small plane and walked in behind me. An older man was there with his pilot clothing on yet reeking of cigarette smoke. He looked capable of flying the plane, I guess.

"So this is the lucky young lady heading to see Mr. Nazir. You ever flown private before Madame," the pilot asked as I settled into a seat near the middle of the plane. "No. This is my first time, Sir," I responded as Charles situated my belongings nearby. "You're in for a treat," the pilot said. Charles was traveling with me. But sat far away and appeared to be doing business work on his laptop in the back of the plane. I wondered if he was doing things for Vincent. The plane took off and we would be in Los Angeles soon.

When we arrived the airport in Los Angeles, there was a town car waiting for me with a sign that said 'Zosia'. I felt it was a tad unnecessary, but enjoyed it anyway. Charles sat in the front of the town car and I in the back, pinching myself casually and saying, "OHMYGODOHMYGODOHMYGOD," on repeat in my head. The scenery from Las Vegas to Los Angeles had no similarities. There were luscious green trees, green hills, and green grass to be seen from the sky while flying overhead in Los Angeles. The same was to be seen from car while passing through the city. There weren't casinos on every corner. Instead there were advertisements on films and the actors in those films. Lavish fashion posters and musical icons adorned the billboards in Los Angeles.

Famous faces you were used to seeing being no more than the size of your hand were now the size of a house and staring at you as you sat at the red light, seductively making eye contact as if to say, "We've been waiting for you to arrive this entire time." Los Angeles had a way of making you feel that it was going to make all of your dreams come true, whatever they were. I felt that energy the moment I entered the smog filled hemisphere. I was ready...

The town car arrived a valet of a large building I assumed were residences. The valet attendant opened my door and greeted me with a bottle of water in his hand.

"Zosia, shall we," Charles stated as I stood absorbing the atmosphere of where I stood. I was consciously tapping into each and every one of my senses so I could remember everything. I wanted to taste the air, hear the traffic and idle chatter of strangers, and the small gust of wind that brushed passed me whenever anyone walked by.

Comfort washed over me immediately and no longer feared what lie ahead as we entered the elevator heading to Vincent's residence.

"How do you like living in Vegas? It's full of opportunities and full of temptation," Charles, Vincent's assistant asked as the elevator's floors rose like a roller-coaster ride. My stomach plummeted. "I like it. And I agree. It definitely is nothing like Nebraska. Much warmer," I laughed as Charles looked at me with his own sense of comfort.

I was lead through a couple secret doors once exiting the elevator. Each door had a unique key that took us to another floor and another door. I felt like I was in 007 and I was being delivered as a gift or on a secret mission. Then Charles assuredly stated, "We're almost there."

He opened the final door and we entered a private elevator with mirrors in it. I imagined myself as Charlie heading to the Chocolate Factory, yet I was the chocolate one in this instance.

The elevator doors opened revealing a double door edged with gold trim and golden handles. It looked regal. I wanted to touch the magical door handle but Charles opened the door for me like the pleasant assistant and gentleman he was. As the door opened, designer furniture and statues from the Renaissance era greeted me. Art adorned the walls, welcoming my presence, and watching me enter with eager eyes. My heart beat faster and I reached to grab my skin so I could pinch it.. again. His home was immaculate. I was in awe. I had never been in a home so elegant.

"What does his heart look like," I wondered.

"Right this way, Zosia, " Charles said loudly as if to announce my presence to Vincent and whomever else was in the home. We entered a dining area where a chef stood beside two tables full of food I knew was prepared for us. Vincent came around the corner of the kitchen holding one glass of wine. He was wearing what appeared to be something he had golfed in earlier that day. But he smelled as if he had just showered. His hair was damp with fresh scent. My vagina muscles clenched as he smiled. The way to my heart was sitting on a table less than 10 feet away, FOOD. Yes, that is when my vagina muscles clenched. The doors didn't do it. The artwork, maybe. The money, nope.

But the aroma that came from the tables ahead was going to write the script for that day.

"Welcome to my home, gorgeous. Allow me to give you a tour before we begin. Shall we," handsome man grabbed my hand with a grip I could have got lost in. It commanded me to attention and made my vagina clench again. His muscles were proudly showing through his shirt. His veins were throbbing in my hand. He kissed my cheek and took me on a tour of the fortress he called home.

"This is for you," Vincent graciously handed me the glass of red wine in his hand. He already knew my favorite things somehow.

"I am very blessed. I take nothing for granted," Vincent concluded, humbly. I liked that. He didn't boast about his wealth. Yet, he toured me his home as if to guide me so that I don't get lost and feel comfortable there. I really liked that. After we ate, I introduced Vincent to some music he had never heard before and helped him set up his Facebook page. He taught me a few things about stocks, bonds, politics, and baseball.

Another glass of my favorite wine.

Now I was giggling and extremely comfortable. His home was full of fancy furniture yet I insisted upon sitting on the floor to chat with him.

"Would you like to go for a swim on the roof? I would love to see you in your bikini again," Vincent seductively asked. With a glass of wine in one hand, I responded, "Sure, but my bikini is in my car. I didn't bring it with me." "One moment. I'll take care of that. Give me your sizes," Vincent said reaching for a notepad and the phone on a table nearby. "What type of car do you have," Vincent asked.

Slightly embarrassed to reveal what type of car I had to this man of great wealth, I slowly responded with my truth, "it's a 2002 Ford Focus and it's my favorite shade of blue."

Charles retrieved a swimsuit from a nearby boutique within what seemed like seconds. There must have been another trap door that he didn't show me.

"Walk for me, gorgeous," Vincent said after I entered the living room with my blue bikini on. I didn't really understand what he meant, but decided to take him very literal and attempted to be as sexy as possible in the heels I didn't really feel like wearing. He approved. Then asked me beside him as he kissed me slowly during a Lykke Li song, I introduced him to. We went to the roof mere steps away overlooking the Los Angeles skyline. There we sat and he kissed me on a patio chair underneath the dream filled sky.

It began to rain. I became smitten with the moment as my bikini bottoms found their way to my knees and his hands found their way to my lap.

He kissed me harder with each stroke of his hand into my lower set of lips. Finally unbuckling his belt quickly as he kissed me with urgency. It rained more. My hair was only slightly damp but I was living out a fantasy I had never thought would ever occur. With every stroke inside of me, he kissed me as if I was his and he was mine.

I felt desired, adored, and needed. I was his Black Playboy Bunny. His Chocolate Goddess. He made me feel like I was the most beautiful woman in the world even though with his money in Las Vegas he had his choice of beautiful women.

"I don't want them. They are empty. I want you because you are full. Full of creativity, intellect, youth, and full of things to teach me. You are real and so are your tits," Vince smirked.

I casually dated Vincent for a few years, pretending not to notice the monetary gifts he left in my purse that I found when I got to my car. I insisted that he didn't have to do that, but he insisted it was for my college fund. Legal prostitution? Perhaps. Fuck. It was Vegas. Live it up. Be as safe as possible. Be the cliché but keep your own morals.

That worked for me. Until I met the man I thought I was going to marry....

CHAPTER: STRANGER LOOKED JUST LIKE ME

It was the end of 1996. I just turned 15. The snow was coming down as if it were rain. The streets were eerily quiet other than the sound of cars breaking as they slid down the icy hill. "Your father is on his way," my mother stated. I looked at the snow outside the window to our townhouse and dreaded what lie ahead. "I have homework. Do I have to go with him," I groaned opening the fridge preparing a glass of milk. "Yes, you do. You only see him a couple times a year. Go be with the Vaugeois'. They're good people," my mother stated. "I know they are, but I don't know them. It's uncomfortable. It always has been. Larry is probably just going to get me another kit of play make up as if I'm a child that likes to play in that garbage. He doesn't know me, mom. He doesn't love me," I said frowning as the cold milk ran down the side of my face.

My mother by now had gone upstairs. The Christmas lights outside began to reveal themselves beneath the snow. The Christmas tree in front of me brought nothing but memories that I wished were warm instead of cold. What's the point in wishing though? Wishing for a family that will never exist.

My father arrived moments later and drove me from Bellevue to North Omaha where Christmas was held at his brother's home, featuring cameos from all of those in the family. Whenever he kissed my cheek, his prickly mustache felt like an intruder upon my cheek. I hated it.

I hated not having a father but having this stranger I was forced to call "Dad". I envied children that simply did not know their father instead of knowing him and knowing that he simply didn't care about you except for on the days when the American calendar tells him to do so.

"Hey Zosia, How have you been," one of my favorite cousins asked. He always made me feel welcome. He and his sister were very sweet. I admired their family life. Their parents were still married. Their father was my father's brother. "I've been good. Happy that this school year is half over and we're on winter break," I stated making small talk yet not wanting to talk too much because he had a speech impediment I could tell made him insecure to speak. The Vaugeois Christmas was hosted at his parent's home every year since our grandmother Dorothy 'Dotsy' died.

I began having flashbacks to going to the Holiday party that my Grandmother hosted for the Omaha community every year. Hundreds of low-income families came to a Christmas themed party where my Uncle dressed as Santa and they gave out toys that were donated from various organizations.

I watched in admiration that I was related to these strangers that looked just like me. I remember telling children that praised them, "That's my grandmother. That's my uncle. That's my dad."

Usually the kids I told didn't believe me, laughed, and ran away. I longed to be a part of their family. I wanted to be VISIBLE.

There I stood, momentarily daydreaming while talking to my favorite cousin. He invited me to sit and watch the rest of the cousins play video games in the dining room. The adult relatives shared memories, none of which featured me. I wanted to tell them something about my childhood so that the fun stories could have me in them too. But I felt foolish and childish for feeling so left out. But I was. I didn't belong there even if every stranger within reach had my eyes, my lips, and my bone structure.

"Zosia, come here I want to introduce you to someone," my father insisted, grabbing my arm with an entitled force that sent a streak of unpleasantness up my spine. He didn't pronounce my name correctly half the time and bossed me around like he had experience changing my diapers at one time. He hadn't. He was just, 'The man that had sex with my mother engaging in half of my creation'. His sense of entitlement always annoyed me. I wanted him to earn me. You can't show up 3 times a year and expect a fatherly bond to magically appear, even if I was his splitting image.

"Who is this beautiful little girl," a woman wearing a brown wig and polyester sweater asked grabbing onto me as if I were a raggedy Ann doll. "This is my daughter Zo-See-Uh," my father said with what looked to be some sort of fake pride. "Zah-Sha, actually," I responded correcting the pronunciation of my name. "Oh Larry, I didn't know you had another daughter. She looks just like you and the other kids. Where has she been hiding," the woman asked still tugging on to my body intrusively. "I haven't been hiding by choice," I thought wondering if my thoughts were loud enough for the room to hear me. I got startled when the look on my father and brown wig's face seemed to suggest as if my thoughts had been given away. "Zah-Sha,.. lives with her mother in Bellevue," my father stated quickly as he segued into another subject to avoid the awkward unspoken questions that came next.

I was 30 years old when my mother told me this: *"Well, my husband was overseas in Japan. I was lonely. Your father was charismatic. He had a play at the Officer's Club on the military base. He starred in it. He directed it. And I thought he was so handsome. He told me he was separated from his wife whom he had 3 children with. I had 3 children too. Mine were all teenagers. Our personal lives had a lot in common. We began to see one another often. Then I got pregnant. Larry asked me to have an abortion but I didn't have the money. I was about four months pregnant when his wife came to my job. July 1981. I was so scared I thought she was going to try to hurt my baby and me. She met me outside by my car and said 'Do you know Larry?'. My heart beat fast and I told her 'Yes, I know him'. As she emerged from behind my car I saw that her stomach was extremely large. She was with child just as I was. I felt sick. She wasn't aggressive or mean at all. Instead she told me "You can have him. He's a piece of shit". We didn't necessarily become friends after that but she called me a few times after you were born when your father was depressed. She thought I could do something about it. She also offered to babysit you a few times as well. But she was still married to Larry and I was scared she may hurt you. She was nice though. Now I know she just wanted to be nice. Back then I wasn't so sure."*

30 years old, I stood in my mother's bedroom and asked, "Why did you get involved with him if you both were married?" "I told you Zosia, he was charming, talented, and said all the right things. You're so much like him in those ways that it's weird. Really really weird. And yet of his 7, you're the child that saw him least," my mother stated as she rolled up her hair.

Flashback to the month before I moved to Vegas.

It was 2009. August.

The phone rang. "Hey Zosia. What time will you and little man be coming by," my cousin asked, preparing for his graduation party. "We will be there as soon as it starts. Do you need me to bring anything," I asked while watching my son play, avoiding the boxes that were already packed. "No, just bring yourself. I'm excited to see you guys," Andrew exclaimed.

"Come on baby. Let's get ready to go."

"Okay mommy. I'm coming," Taylor said putting up his toys and smiling at me in the way that made my heart fill up with purpose.

CHAPTER: PURPOSE

According to my mother, I began writing as soon as I could talk and tell a story. She said I would write whatever story I wanted to tell in scribbles on a piece of paper and read it to whomever would listen. I've always found this amusing, because I am still this way. In 3rd grade, my teacher Mrs. Long fell in love with my stories and realized they entertained the class. I was shy however. So she pushed me out of that and showed me that I was making others laugh, smile, and think. I fell in love with being in front of an audience with my voice and my message. Every day after lunch, she allowed me to read my 'Monster' stories in front of the class. Writing about the monsters that were in my dreams, I thought would make them go away.

They did not.

CHAPTER: SUCCUBUS

It's amazing how connected we all are. You sometimes do not realize the purpose of a relationship in your life until that relationship is over. Some people are placed in our lives simply as guides towards our destiny or toward other people we are supposed to meet in order to be a guide for them.

I was in LA, driving to a photo shoot with a photographer I had known of and communicated with for 5 or 6 years when I was still living in Nebraska. The thirties are when you understand the mistakes from your 20's and hopefully have gained some wisdom from those experiences.

Phone rings. It was Van. "So here's the schedule, boob. I have to do some errands for work but I do want to see you," Van spoke swiftly as I drove down Highland through Hollywood, admiring my future home adorned with Palm trees, graffiti, dreams, and traffic. "That's fine. I'm almost done reading that script you gave me and I will finish my notes probably when I am back in Vegas. I am heading to a shoot now," I replied anxiously because I knew he wanted a deadline. "Can you get it done tonight," Van asked.

"No, I cannot. I have other things to do. I do not mind helping you, but I came here on business and still have my own responsibilities to tend to before I can do yours."

Van was always doing something. He wished to be a film or television producer. When I met him, I admired his organization skills and lust for the same industry as I. I thought one day, he might produce a film that I wrote. I was hoping we would one day be a husband and wife team. But 2 months before now, I had given up on this dream. Or at least the part that included him. I was nothing more than his unpaid Hollywood assistant. I did what I did out of love. The only thing I got in return was him talking to me like I was a child and belittling me when I asked a question about a task that he wanted me to do. Yet, still, I couldn't say no. I just wasn't quite as eager as I was a year ago when I was booking his flights, submitting him to castings, doing minor production assistant duties, making him a website, sending him gifts, and sucking his imaginary dick. Figuratively because Van was abstinent too. At least that's what I believed.

A few days prior I had a meet and greet with Scott. He wanted to meet me before our shoot for one of his upcoming magazines. I secretly thought it was so he could make sure I looked like my pictures/videos online. I had no problem with that. You cannot really know what someone looks like until you are with them face to face. Energy is something that is not easily transferred through the Internet.

Scott had worked as a producer himself recently on a major film.
I was greeted with the film poster as I walked in.
"Hey Miss Zosia. It's so nice to finally meet you," Scott hugged me and I was enamored by his southern accent that I was not expecting.

The day of the shoot, I had a lot on my mind. *I was 31 years old. How much longer did I have to use modeling as a crutch into the entertainment industry. Las Vegas did not provide the opportunities for Black models that LA did. Yet, LA was completely saturated with talent of all kinds. I still wanted to live there, here, in LA. Yet, the income I was making versus my rent in Las Vegas was a steal in comparison to anything I felt I would ever find in LA. Single mother splitting the rent with someone else in Vegas is $400 + for one room. Los Angeles I couldn't imagine would be as generous or reasonable. A studio apartment in a nice area in LA was at least $1,000 a month. I couldn't afford that! I still had a child to take care of.* Frustrated, I focused on the possibilities instead of the problems and kept driving through Hollywood towards my shoot.

Parking in Korea-town was just as difficult as anywhere else in LA. You had to read the signs and make sure you would have a car when you finished conducting whatever business you had. And if you did still have a car and weren't towed, you had to make sure you didn't have a $75 dollar ticket on your window. I found a spot. I threw my bags over my shoulder and drug my suitcase behind me, while taking in the area for memory and for reference of future possible residences. I was STOKED to shoot with Scott.

His significant other Jenille, would be doing my hair and make up. I tapped on the door greeted by Jenille. She was a bubbly joy. The dynamic of having a photographer for a boyfriend intrigued me from an observation point of view.

We shot all day long. That evening I drove to

Venice beach where Van lived. I wanted to surprise him. I was in love with him after all. In hindsight, I should have called him first. I heard some noises leading to his penthouse but I thought it was the television. The door wasn't locked, so I went in. On the counter was takeout that looked like it hadn't been touched. The bags were still moist with the humidity from being cooked.

The grunts coming from the bedroom got louder as I walked up the stairs. I locked eyes with two naked men, both facing the door, connected at the waist.

"Z. I um.. I thought you were still shooting," Van mumbled, grabbing a sheet to cover him as his male friend looked on like he had seen a ghost.

"I finished and.. wanted to surprise you."

"Oh you surprised him alright," the male model stated with a smile and a rub of the brow.

"Shut up, Quincy," Van retorted, embarrassed.
The signs were all there. We never had sex with one another, but I thought that he was just saving it for Jesus… Depending on how you read that it could be the Spanish version of another male model hiding under the bed that day and not the Lord his savior. But I digress. He just wasn't the one.

I collected what was left of my dignity and showed myself out. The porno I had just walked in on was replaying over in my head and I needed a cleanse. LaLa's Grill on Sunset was the closet thing I could think of to get a drink and a new meal as I left my other one on Van's countertop. I imagined Van, Quincy, and Jesús hand feeding one another the take out I purchased. Oh well. I hoped it was delicious, with two sides of dick.

Driving down Sunset Blvd, blasting my music as loud as possible, I pulled up to my restaurant of choice. I sat alone at the bar inside.

"Excuse me, mind if I join you," a gentle eyed gentleman asked. "Sure," I replied skeptical of his intent but intrigued by his candor. He wore flashy clothes and his teeth were as white as the purest cocaine. "What's your name," he asked. "Z," I said, hoping he wouldn't ask for clarification. "Z, Wow, I am Z too," he smiled. I knew who he was. I was listening to his music in the car on my way there. But I played along as not to feed his ego or seem to be overly impressed with his celebrity status.

I assumed celebrities all expected to be endlessly praised for just existing. I'd be damned before giving him that disingenuous satisfaction. Seeing a celebrity in LA wasn't uncommon or even impressive. It was just a part of life there. Zeppelin and I chat for a while and exchanged numbers. He told me he had a show in Las Vegas the following week and was going to come to see me.

It was surreal being pursued by one of my favorite musicians. But he was still a musician. I had to be careful. Naiveté would not be my downfall.

The day before he came to Las Vegas, the biggest bouquet of stargazer lilies arrived. My entire home was pierced with their elegant scent and I, smitten.

In Vegas we spent the entire week together. He had some time off between shows and dedicated it all to me. I was falling fast. And it seemed he was too. When I returned home, the flowers he sent me had finally bloomed.

"I've arranged a flight for you to come to LA to meet my family," Zeppelin stated as we lay in the biggest suite I've ever been in. Superstardom had its perks, I guess. Every so often, I pinched myself in disbelief that this was my life. He began writing mini songs about me. Then leaving his sexy raspy voice in my voicemail. Still abstinent, I began to yearn for him to be inside of me in all the ways. Decided it would be him that made my flower bloom again.

I wanted someone to work for it, prove their loyalty, and protect my heart. Once you learn that your heart and vagina are connected, they both need condoms to be properly protected. That's how it was, at least for me.

Driving my car to the Vegas airport to park for daily parking is so convenient if you only plan to be gone for a few days. No taxi, no bull-shit, no flaky friends. I parked in the temporary parking, and head to my first Virgin Atlantic flight.

"Where you headed," the gentleman sharing my armrest asked. "LA," I smiled. "Final destination," he inquired. "Yes, unless you're talking about that scary ass movie where everything that could go wrong goes wrong… flights for instance," I laughed. "Oh. Yeah. No. No. Not that. You're funny. So what's in LA," he further asked placing his phone on airplane mode. "A friend lives there," I responded simply. "Oh. That kind of friend," the gentleman teased. "How can you tell? I didn't smile or anything," I asked. "Your eyes. Your eyes tell more than your mouth does. And I see love in your eyes. Be careful with that. Love is a dangerous thing. Love has the power to bring every other emotion to attention," he finished.

Once I was off of the airplane, I could already feel the wet, pleasant change in climate. Being near an ocean was different in ways that I craved, especially with my current residence in the desert. My skin, hair, and soul felt alive.
I began to wonder if the dry desert had the same effect on my sex life.

His sister and brother picked me up from the Burbank airport, promptly. His flight was arriving across town at LAX. "So, how do you know Zeppelin," Tina asked. "We met at a restaurant. I was there alone and so was he," I blushed. "He has been talking about you nonstop," Jeff said, turning to face me from the passenger seat.

"Oh really? I've been doing a lot of the same."

"The family is really excited to meet you. Mom and Dad are coming over later with some friends," Tina said, getting on the 405 freeway toward LAX.

Inner monologue started to calm my anxiety of meeting the family. Meeting the family in new relationships is a milestone. You have to make a good impression, be yourself, and not openly show that you're fucking the shit out of their son. It's a complicated dichotomy that I was walking into. One of Zeppelin's songs came on the radio as we drove. I gazed on as we all rocked to the beat.

We arrived at LAX and there Zeppelin was waiting at the passenger pick up, incognito. The windows in the backseat were so tinted that I could hardly see him. When in love, our lovers become gods. They are a celebrity all their own.

Butterflies rose in my stomach, my hands got sweaty, and like a schoolgirl crush, I tried to hide the excitement from seeing my 'superstar'. Being with him made me feel like I was on another planet, but not alone this time.

Weeks passed. Nightfall came quickly as it always did. I dreamt that I was naked and running through a labyrinth from a woman that looked just like me but more attractive. It seemed as if she knew which direction I was going to go with more ease as time went on in the dream. The faster I ran, the slower she had to run because I was too busy looking back at her, I was making mistakes.

Finally, I got to where I thought was an exit and she jumped out in front of me. Her eyes were the deepest black I'd ever seen. Her teeth started to grow out of her mouth like sharp talons. I reached to touch her and she morphed from beautiful girl, to Succubus, to demon. The initial jolt of shock being face to face with this demon immediately woke me with my own scream as she reached her final form.

"Z, you alright," Zeppelin asked as we lay in his bed. Lying in a pool of my own cold sweat, embarrassed and still frightened by my own mind, I whispered, "Yes, I think so." "What were you dreaming about," Zeppelin inquired, exposing his bright curious eyes. I was too ashamed to tell him about this recurring dream I had been having.
To give him all the details of this dream would reveal the dark parts of myself to him.

Inner monologue began, "Zosia, are you going to tell him or should we?"

"It was nothing. Clowns," I laughed, while lying through my teeth. "Clowns, like Pennywise, Tim Curry clown or Homey the Clown," Zeppelin asked, making fun. "Like a Zeppelin Wolf clown," I joked as we kissed and began throwing pillows.

Drugs are a part of the lifestyle for a lot of artists and entertainers. At least that's what you're expected to think and tolerate when you meet one with a drug problem. They'll tell you anything from, "This is the last time, this helps me create number one albums, I make love to you better, to I know it's going to kill me, I've accepted that." And no matter how many times you find them black out drunk, or up for 52 hours straight because they were combining all of the opiates that they could find, you have a hard time walking away. Because love makes fools of us all. And some of us want so bad to help that we lose ourselves in the process.

When the heroin wore off, he moved on to Lortabs or hydrocodone tablets. Zeppelin said it was for his pain this time. But when you're standing there watching someone kill themselves slowly, you begin to hate everyone else around enabling him.

Then you begin to wonder if you too are also enabling him by staying with him and agreeing to watch his extreme highs become overshadowed because he's become dependent on his opiate cocktail.

Zepp had a few shows in Europe. I came for his last night in London. "Babe, will you get that," Zeppelin stated as we sat backstage in his dressing room. Someone had just knocked on his door in the midst of his desperate drug withdrawal. I opened the door and it was his bodyguard and dealer, Jake. I hated his guts. I don't even have to tell you why.

"Is it all in there, my guy," Zeppelin asked, breathing heavily as he felt for the brown paper sack. "Yes, I even got him to get you and the lady some molly for later," Jake stated. Jake looked like what a Russian Steve Urkel would look like if he was also drinking steroids with his Wheaties and milk every morning. He was loyal & strong but guided by greed. His loyalty was to do whatever the millionaire said to do, even if it could potentially kill him.

I watched Zeppelin and his band perform on the stage that night. He kept messing up. It killed me. A man that could play every instrument and sing in every key, looked like the drunk guy that got lost and ruined karaoke on someone's wedding night. I was tired of arguing with him on whether or not his 20K a month habit was going to be the death of him. But I decided, I wasn't going to let loving him be the death of me.

I head to the airport to catch the next flight back to Las Vegas.

The next time I would see Zeppelin Wolf was as he was accepting his Grammy, a year later. His eyes; no longer gentle, no longer honest, had gone black.

CHAPTER: LUCK, BE A LADY

"Waffles and 6 slices of bacon please," I said to the waiter as Jane stared decisively at the menu. "And for you miss," the waiter asked as the Vegas sun beamed into Jane's eyes. "I'll take the Southwestern Omelet please. Annnnnnd could you put some salsa on the side," Jane finished with a smug grin.

This was Jane's first trip to Vegas. I hadn't seen her since I left Nebraska and was happy to show her what life outside of the cornfields was like. We sat outside in a cabana and ended up with some of the promotional team from Peppermint Hippo. I had not been at Peppermint Hippo for very long at this point, but some of the girls knew who I was. Muse. Jane was still getting used to the idea that I was trying my hand at gambling. And by gambling I mean showing strangers my tits. I liked to attest that Vegas hadn't changed me. It just simply brought about more options and the ability to choose between them.

"What do you want to do tonight? I was thinking we could go downtown? This cute guy on Facebook invited me to see his band at a lounge. It's live music. We can dance and stuff like old times. But it's totally up to you. I told him I may not be able to make it because my best friend was in town," I smiled between bites. "Oh? I love live music. What type of music is it," Jane asked. "I'm not quite sure.

From the looks of it, it looks like Lounge Singer type of music but they apparently play original songs and popular covers which I think is really impressive. I've never met the Facebook guy before, but his eyes look honest," I replied recalling his mental image.

"Let's do it," Jane said without emotion.

Later that evening we reached one of the older casinos in Old Vegas called, 'The Sinatra'. Every night there was a different band or performer in the main lounge hoping to get a gig at one of the larger casinos or perhaps even a record deal.

There were 7 of them. 5 brothers and 2 sisters in a 7-piece band called Moonshine. The youngest was the sister; Isa (Isabella) who played the violin. Isa was funky and sassy like a cross between a rock star and librarian. Then there was Giovanni on the Electric guitar. Osanna played the cello but knew her way around the rest of the strings as well. Pasquale played the saxophone and was the oldest. You could see the discernment and loyalty to his family in his eyes. Valentino played the trumpet and had a smile that lit up the entire room. Luciano knew how to play a little bit of everything. He looked up to their father who also knew his way around a stage and was an orchestra teacher.

Nico however was the lead vocalist and piano player; the star of the show. He was like a modern day Elvis mixed with Ray Charles, Chubbie Checker, and Frank Sinatra.

His full deep brunette hair was flawless and I was scared to death of him the moment he laid his eyes on me.

As Jane and I entered the lounge, the band was in the middle of song. My eyes met with Giovanni first. It was Giovanni who invited me after all. Giovanni's glasses titled at the brim of his eye and he gave a nod that he saw me without skipping a beat in song. The electricity of everyone's energy passed through me as Jane and I made our way closer to the front of the room where the band played. Immediately we began dancing along as the music played, allowing our dresses to fly with the notes, and teleport us back to the 1950's. 1950's minus the racism.

"He's cute, Zosia," Jane giggled looking towards the young man that invited us to see his band. "Which one? They're all ridiculously good looking. Gio is really cute though. But he's kind of boney. I need a man with some meat on his bones other than sausage," I whispered with a laugh.

Nico, while singing & playing the piano, made an intent of maintaining eye contact with me. He then pulled the mic off the stand and came over to me. While still in song, he pulled the microphone away from his mouth, handed me a napkin and whispered, "Put your number down."

What the fuck? I haven't even had a conversation with this handsome jackass and he's asking me to put my number down… in front of EVERYONE. I looked up at Giovanni who played his instrument without any concerns of the outside world. Then back at the fresh napkin that sat beside my glass of wine. The band played on, enthusiastically being lost in the music they created together. Nico had made his way back to the stage but made sure to keep his eyes on me.

"Ooooh Zosia. What was that? Do you know him too," Jane asked instigating the exchange that just occurred between myself and the charismatic lounge singer.

"No. I DON'T know him. And that was weird. I'm ready to go," I said rolling my eyes with distaste. Sure, Nico was incredibly good looking. Did I say that already? But there was a blatant arrogance there that didn't even bother being bashful while crossing the line from Confidence Street. He didn't look both ways, he just crossed with reckless abandon.

"What? I think he's just being fun. Looks like everyone here is having a good time. He's the cutest of them all," Jane giggled with her inhibitions let down. I could tell she was living vicariously through me since she had recently moved in with her lover. "Yeah. I suppose. All fun and games huh? Good ole' Vegas life,"

I smiled scanning the stage and magically making eye contact with each one of the members of the D'Elia family.

After the show, each member of the band came and introduced themselves. It was pleasant. Nico held my hand a little longer than was comfortable during our shake and Giovanni saved himself for last as he was the one I wanted to speak with the most. Like an inquisitive child, Giovanni scanned every response I gave him during our conversation. Attempting to look through me for perhaps his own agendas or maybe Nico's...

Jane and I stumbled to my car that working at Peppermint Hippo had suddenly afforded me. Drinking and driving in Las Vegas was just as dangerous as any other city, but seemed to be more common. I wasn't shit faced by any means, but did feel like I was living on a dream as the lights from the Las Vegas strip lit our way back to Jane's hotel.

"Your life seems to be good here Zosh," Jane said twirling her hair as she lay near my feet on her hotel bed. "Yeah. It definitely improved once I left the Midwest for sure. And don't get me wrong. I'm not trying to put down Nebraska. Not completely. But so many people there have big dreams and are too afraid to leave their comfort zone and pursue them. It doesn't have to be a dream in entertainment or something flashy. A dream is a dream.
And if you dream of leaving, you should do that," I said with a wink.

Jane sighed and sat up, "I hear you, but what about…". "What about what? Nothing. If I can do it with the challenges I had, anyone can. It really just takes shutting that little voice inside your head out that says you can't… and tell it you can and to shut the fuck up," I laughed.

"The only person that can truly convince you that you CANNOT is you. So as Yoda said.. 'Do or do not. There is no try'. If you don't want to be there anymore, fucking leave."

"Alright. I get it," Jane snapped, tired of my drunken encouragement poster speech.

"That family was gorgeous. Could you imagine an orgy with all 7 of them? I could," I whispered as Jane fell off the side of the bed in laughter. "Yes, I could see it," Jane chuckled. "Which position am I in," I asked.

"Z, you need help," Jane laughed.

"Jane, you have no idea."

CHAPTER: DISNEYLAND

It's four-thirty am and I'm sitting on my bathroom floor hugging a dead man's shoe. It smells just like him. His feet are going to have to be enough. I made mental note of them just a couple of months ago. I can hear his voice between my sobs as I attempt not to wake the neighbors whom I'm not even sure exist anymore. They're never home.

Flashback to a month ago:

"Your whole face smiles. Did you know that?" I asked, as Nuru held me with his arms in his kitchen. He was cooking that night. His long black mane effortlessly glowed in the darkness as I tried to hide my smile beneath my bowing head tilt.

"Yeah. I knew. You like it?" Nuru asked as he massaged my shoulders. "Of course I do," I blushed. "Your smile reminds me of Tommy Lee Jones. Do you know who he is? I told myself if I ever found a smile like his, I would never let it go," I giggled. "Oh yeah? Well then I suggest you don't let me go. Not ever," Nuru responded, looking intently into my eyes in the way that makes your soul stand at attention as if he's trying to tell you something he refuses to say aloud.

Finally, I found the love I sought in this man's smile, eyes, and embrace. Everything was looking up. Life was finally going my way.

I woke up in the middle of the night and went to the bathroom at the end of the hall. Nuru was sitting on the steps grabbing his head violently and mumbling something to himself. "Babe," I whispered, "is everything okay?"

"I need you to go away. You're not supposed to be here. You're interfering with some things I have planned. I am going to end up hurting you if you stay with me," Nuru scoffed.

"What? What is it? Let me help you."

"You cannot help me."

"What do you want me to do?"

"Nothing. I don't want you to do anything. I shouldn't have started this relationship with you, Z. The voices. They don't want you here."

"Voices? What voices, Nuru?"

I began to cry watching the madness take him over and he stormed down the stairs, out of view, and left the house.

The next day, a group of us drove to Disneyland. It had been years since I had seen the Magic Kingdom.

"What do you want to ride first," Nuru asked, never letting go of my hand. "EVERYTHING and then you," I smiled, gently squeezing his hand back.

"Oh, you want to ride me too? I can make that happen. But first let's ride Space Mountain."

Nuru seemed happy that day, but I couldn't help but think of the sadness in his eyes the day before and wonder what it all meant. Was there someone else? Was I not enough? The voices in MY head started to talk.

We spent the day goofing off like children at the magical themed park where everything seemed perfect. Disneyland had a similar effect on adults that it did on children. But once you left the property, you had to return to whatever reality you came from.

Nuru had another episode at the hotel where he screamed at me. It was unlike him. I didn't know what I did wrong or what I should say to calm him, so I left him alone.

"Z, are you sure you want to be with him, " Karen asked in the hotel room as Nuru's male friends comforted him outside. Before I answered her question, I considered whether or not I could deal with whatever this was that he was going through. Then I told myself that maybe I finally found someone just as fucked up as me and would be a fool to turn my back on him.

"Yes. I want to be with him. (I love him)," I said, plainly. "Good. He needs you. He needs someone good," Karen stated between full breaths, taking a hit of the marijuana pipe.

The following morning, a group of us walked to the beach to lie out for the day.

"This is really beautiful. Just laying here with you as the sun sets over the ocean. My favorite place on Earth. You. Here. Now," I said lying on Nuru's bulky chest covered with his long black mane.

"I'm really happy you're here. Thank you for being here...," Nuru smiled.

"Thank you for having me. I almost want to take a picture of this. But a picture won't capture what we see..."

"Want to take some? I don't mind."

"Naa. Let's not ruin the moment with technology. We can take some with our brain. Memories are much better," I replied.

Nuru animated his hands and whispered, "Click. Click. Click. How's that?"

"Perfect."

As the days progressed, Nuru became distant. As he became distant, my worries grew and I considered giving him space to figure things out, unaware of what was plaguing him.

It was Monday again. I was hired on the

production team for a movie that was being filmed in Las Vegas. One of the producers recognized me and wanted to give me a walk on role with a couple of lines. While I was heading to wardrobe, I saw him.

"Nuru! Hey," I exclaimed from the trailer. Nuru ran up to me and whisked me off of my feet with a kiss that made the hair on my legs grow back. I was taken back by his kiss as the last time I saw him, he was … different. But his kiss reassured me that things were going to be okay.

"You want to come by later?" Nuru asked. "Yes. Of course. What time," I asked, delighted. "Midnight. Come by at midnight. I'll cook for you. Come to me."

Exhausted, I rang the doorbell at exactly midnight. Nuru opened the door slightly and walked away before I could see him fully. We met at the couch where he sat with tears streaming down his face.

"What's wrong, Nuru? Please let me in. I'm not going anywhere unless you want me to," I pleaded.

"You wouldn't understand. No one understands," Nuru whispered, attempting to hide his pain.

"I'm trying to understand, but you won't let me in. What is it? I am your friend."

"That's just it. I don't think I can be a good boyfriend, friend, or anything to you right now. I'm going to end up hurting you if you stay with me.

You came at a strange point in my life. This wasn't supposed to happen. You're interfering with some things I have planned... and I don't want to hurt you."

"Nuru, You told me that already. I am here in whatever capacity you allow. You lead and I'll follow you wherever you want to go," I assured him.

"Anywhere?" Nuru, asked.

"Yes."

"How do you feel about Hawaii," Nuru asked.

"I'm obsessed with it, but have never been," I responded.

"Then that's where we will go," he smiled.

The conversation shifted quickly.

"Have you ever spoken to the dead? Like do you think that you could," Nuru asked, plainly.

"I've never tried. I don't know. Is it possible?"

"I think you have it in you to," Nuru smiled.

"I suppose if I were connected enough to someone that passed away, I could maybe, I said.

"YOU DEFINITELY CAN," Nuru said, grabbing a coconut water.

"What are your dreams, Zosia?"

"I want to be happy. I want to influence the world somehow in a positive way; I suppose even if by my own self-discovery; I also inflict a great deal of pain on myself, " I said nuzzled into his shoulder.

"That book you dream or writing. I think this will be it." he said with a look of omniscient assurance.

I chuckled at the dominance and certainty in his voice; promising so convincingly that he knew. He said, "Whatever is the strongest on your heart is something that you already knew."

A couple of nights later, I arrived at Nuru's home at midnight again. He greeted me in a way he never had before. He kissed me with an urgent passion like he would never see me again. It wasn't sexual, it was …magical. While it felt like a Disney scene, I knew something wasn't right. Immediately, he began ripping my clothes off in the sexiest way, never breaking eye contact.

Nuru then proceeded to make love to me in a way no one had ever made love to me before. I was bleeding yet he did not care and kissed my love pocket, and drank the river of me as if the juices from my body were giving him life. No objection. No disgust. Craving. Desire. REAL LOVE. He placed me atop of him, and for the first time, it was me that could not look into his eyes. I kept looking away, for no reason I could understand on a conscious level. He grabbed my face and forced me to look into his eyes as tears rolled down my cheeks.

___

Sobbing and violently throbbing upon his love muscle, I cried and he pierced my eyes with his. He connected to a place beyond my eyes. Exhausted we collapsed into one another's embrace.

"What was that," I whispered.

"What was what, " he asked.

"Why was I crying just now? What did you show me in your eyes," I asked, spooked and mesmerized.

"I don't know. What did you see?"

"I saw something. I know I did. You showed me something just now. I cannot describe it. But … I want to know."

"They're louder than you are. The voices… Nothing, Z. It was nothing," Nuru turned away.

"The voices? What voices, babe," I asked.

Confused, I sat up on the bed as the rain started to pour over the desert.

"Are you okay to drive home," Nuru asked.

"What do you mean?"

"I need to be alone now," Nuru quipped, seeming angry that I discovered something. His long mane glowed in the dim room as he stood up, displaying his majestic muscular body.

With the moon over his shoulder, I took a picture with my mind.

He stopped looking into my eyes. As if HE was afraid to look at me. He would come close to looking and stare somewhere else to avoid them.

We got to my car as the tightness hit my throat. This was the first time he was sending me home. I knew that he needed me there, but I wasn't going to be anywhere unwelcome. Whether it was for love or not.

I sat in my car seat, hesitating to put my entire body into the car with the door open as he stood outside. The rain stopped.

"Is there anything else you want to say," I asked.

"Goodnight, Zosia, I... I'll see you later," Nuru whispered, kissing me slowly on my forehead like a child he would never see again. He made sure to leave his lips on my 'third eye' for a moment. Though soothing, I wanted his lips on my mouth. The insecurity in me craved reassurance that everything was okay.

I knew something was up and decided not to bite my tongue.

"I don't want to leave you," I said adamantly protesting like a child whose fun had come to an end.

I saw tears in his eyes... Before they fell, he turned and walked away.

My heart dropped to my stomach as I watched his strong walk disappear into the darkness. His tribal tattoos danced across his shirtless body and bare feet. Taking pictures of him with my tear filled eyes, I finally drove off. Attempting to drown out my thoughts, I played our favorite song by The XX. My soul mate was hurting... and I couldn't do anything about it.

Sometimes when I looked at Nuru, I saw two people. And I was irrevocably in love with them both.

Days passed. I still hadn't heard from Nuru. I wanted to give him some space. It was his turn to reach out. Afraid to lose him forever, I thought there might be someone else. I didn't care. I still wanted him in my life.

There was someone else... They just weren't human. Forces stronger than I were interfering between this world and the next one. Shadows. Spirits.

It had now been 3 weeks since I had heard his soothing voice. In my mind I scheduled the day I was going to make him dinner and invite him over to talk.

I woke up from a nightmare about Nuru. Even in my dreams I could not escape him. I began talking to him, through myself in his absence.

"Please call me. I'm here for you," I would say to myself hoping the spirits would deliver the message to him somehow.

I received a call that Nuru was missing. Immediately I went into panic thinking he had fallen during a hike on one of his favorite trails on Red Rock Mountain in Las Vegas. They said he told them he was going to Hawaii but his phone was off.

Come to me...

Flustered, I too attempted to call his phone. Voicemail. His soothing voice comforted me for 3 seconds. I went to my cabinet and found a bottle of whiskey. I began drinking profusely. Coping mechanism. Functioning alcohol was going to get me through the day...

CHAPTER: BLEEDING

"PLEASE. PLEASE," I begged as my husband began hitting me. He morphed into a monster during his attacks. No longer the sweet airman I had met a year prior. "I heard you in your sleep. You were dreaming of someone. I know it," he stammered, slapping me across my lips in what seemed slow motion as the spit flew out my mouth and mixed with my won blood. Our 3-month-old baby sat quietly in his play-seat, near my high school backpack. "I don't know what you're talking about. I cannot help my dreams. Please stop hitting me. The baby, he can hear us," 18 year old me whispered. "You want to leave me don't you? That's all you talk about. Leaving me. You're not going ANYWHERE," Anthony yelled, throwing me into the glass table as it shattered.

I had a breakthrough. For the first time I decided to fight back. I wasn't going to go die this way. Using all my teenage angst, motherly instinct, and fear, I knocked him on his ass. He then grabbed me by the neck, began choking me, and threw me into the glass table. Shattered glass went everywhere, barely missing our infant son as he watched in silence. I wondered if on some level his calm baby demeanor was to keep the peace in the already volatile home he was born into. Skin cut with glass, tears in my eyes, I stared at the monster I lived with.

He grabbed me by the back of the neck and threw me into the closet, locking it with a chair. I could hear my baby babble in the background as I heard him pick him up out of his play seat.

"Look what you made me do, Zosia. He's scared of me now. You MADE ME DO THIS. YOU MADE ME. You keep trying to leave me. Stay there for a while," Anthony stated as I heard the front door to our military townhouse slam.

In the darkness of the closet, I sat and thought of what I would do to get away from him. I had no one to call that I felt gave enough of a fuck to help me. I also was determined to finish my senior year of high school without having to go to a battered woman's shelter.

My resources were limited but my faith trudged on.

Every other day it was something else that angered him to the point of punches, pinches, and slams.

One night we were arguing and he brought the biggest knife he could find, took it to my neck, threatening to kill our son and me if I dared leave him.

A knock appeared at the door. He placed the knife under a pillow on the living room couch.

I wiped the tears from my face and he motioned

for me to open the door.

For the first time during our relationship, I saw fear in HIS EYES. This told me that I had to put on my fake persona and pretend that everything was fine.

Out the door were two military police officers. They came in and asked how our night was going. I smiled and said, "fine." One of the officers then separated us. One took Anthony into the living room and the other took me into the kitchen to talk to us away from one another.

"Ma'am. What is going on here," the patient officer asked.

"Nothing. We were just about to make dinner," I lied, protecting the man who I feared. "You can tell me the truth. He cannot hear you in here," the man assured me, whispering and taking me deeper into the kitchen.

"Come with me," he said, escorting me back into the living room where the other officer stood with Anthony.

The second officer detained Anthony, while the other officer lifted the pillow, revealing the knife that lay beneath it. "We were walking by, heard a disturbance, and listened at the door for a good while before we knocked. We heard everything.

You're coming with us," the bigger officer stated as they handcuffed Anthony.

"I didn't do anything," Anthony protested. "She's my wife. I would never hurt her."

Anthony's eyes appeared to ask me for help. But I had already lied. There was nothing left I could do. They found his weapon and escorted Anthony out of the door. A military restraining order is called a 'No Contact' order. They handled their issues with the airman separate from the local police department if the issue occurred on the military base.

I flashback to the night, I was awakened by Anthony sitting atop of me as I slept. He began punching me in the face as I slept. Waking up to that is quite the sight. Sleeping when our lives are most vulnerable. I then began to sleep with a knife under my pillow, prepared to slash his neck if he ever disturbed my slumber again. I knew jail was a possibility for murder. But I hoped, I prayed, that God would finally let me free.

Looking down at my arm as the police took him away, I watched the blood drip... Bleeding on the inside, more than what they could see.

CHAPTER: SEVERED HEAD

Though Nuru was missing for the passed 48 hours, I had hope that he would be found. I envisioned him just clearing his head, lost away from technology, which he claimed was the NSA. He was unplugged. He deserved to be unplugged for a few days. If only more of us were brave enough to take that plunge and be away from our phones and shut off social media for a little while. Yet, in this society, most of the youth and elders were chasing superficial love in the form of 'likes', 'follows', and 'retweets'.

Nuru never needed any of that validation. He simply existed and people liked him, followed him, and quoted what he was saying. He was the opposite of everything superficial about the current ways of society. He resented the disingenuous ways of the world. Nuru was a gentle giant with a heart of gold, the physique of a super-hero gladiator, and the mane of a noble steed.

Whenever I imagined him, I saw him in my mind as the glorious human that he was. His entire face smiled, from his brow to his chin, full of deep skin wrinkles whenever he smiled. It was impossible for him to do it any other way. So when Becky texted me from Spain to tell me that Nuru had just killed himself, I fell to the floor.

It took only 6 seconds to rev the engine on his black 1970 Mustang Boss up to 60 miles per hour.

At 93 miles per hour, Nuru whispered his last words, and pulled full speed ahead off the cliff into the darkness over the ocean cliffs as the hibiscus wreaths from his backseat showered his severed head. The hood flew open, ripped off through the glass and took his head with it.

Reading her words through the text messaging service, the world around me went from something familiar to a land I had never been. It was better she told me this way. Written word allowed me to process without a need for the reply that I was not prepared to give immediately. I could hear the intricate rhythm of my broken heartbeat shake my entire core. There on the floor, I still laid in a ball of despair. I responded back, "Please don't let this be true. Are you sure?"

Denial began to take over. I started bargaining with God in my head. Asking him to make it be a mistake. Nuru appeared to me as a spirit of light several times between my sobs. Some friends tried to convince me that his ghost was created out of grieving. I was convinced that I saw him. He was with me. I had to hide my visions from my colleagues because I feared they would think I was crazy. Was I? Is mental illness contagious? Or had I always been insane?

I was awake for 72 hours after hearing the news of his death. I couldn't eat. Sleep was impossible. Grief is an emotion that brings every emotion to the surface. I was jealous of those that had spent more time with him than I had. In pain, that I couldn't see the signs.

In love that never got a chance to fully blossom. In between imagining his body flying through the windshield of his car, I knew I would never be the same. Zosia was gone forever.

When someone kills themselves, there are so many stigmas associated with mental illness. Most of them are inaccurate. The religious will say that the person is going to hell for taking their own life and playing God. Others will say, "At least he's not hurting anymore. He's in a better place." Some pontificate that suicide is a coward's act. This is not true. To take your life requires tremendous courage. No one knows for sure what or if anything exists after this life. What if you fail and end up paralyzed or institutionalized and thus making things worse than before attempting to end your pain? It's hard to know what will happen when your mind turns against you and tells you that you no longer belong on earth. Inevitably, we all eventually die.

There's a saying that says, "be careful what you put up with. You become capable of doing whatever is repeatedly done to you. Enabling monsters will turn you into one."

Masturbating to the memory of a dead man with his shirt in my hand. All while ashamed after each orgasm that no living human could give me.
I had become my own Incubus. I had become the monster I feared the most.

"Nuru, if you can hear me, please show yourself. No. Wait," I hesitated afraid of what I would see. Would he be as he was when I saw him last or would he be covered in blood the way that he passed?

My mind began playing tricks on me. I was seeing things that couldn't possibly be there. It was as if talking to Nuru opened a portal to another dimension and since I was willing to listen, the other dimension were willing to 'talk'. Not everything that came from these other dimensions was pleasant. Some of the visions I saw were dark. Like shadowy figures with eyes that are always there watching. And when they aren't in plain view, your peripheral catches them just out of sight enough to know that something was just there.

CHAPTER: DESIDERIUM

"How do you feel about Hawaii," Nuru asked.

"I'm obsessed with it, but have never been," I
responded.

The voices became like shadows. No matter how
much I tried to escape them, when darkness fell,
there they were telling me that I did not belong here.
Like the dark lullaby by Radiohead, I felt like a
'Creep', an outsider in the world that was so cruel.

Come to me...

There I sat in the LAX airport, holding my
passport. A few feet away my eyes met with one of
my Las Vegas commercial ads. I looked at my own
smiling face and saw a stranger. Staring off into
space, I began daydreaming of the desert fire that
took place a few nights prior. The fire-grilled pizza
nearby dragged my olfactory senses to the fiery
memory.

"Good morning, passengers. We are now
boarding Flight 333 to Honolulu," the young man
said over the intercom. I gathered my small bag and
began to head to the gate.
Arriving Hawaii looked like the first stage of REM
sleep where everything doesn't seem real. It was
more beautiful than any picture or video I have ever
seen.

CHAPTER: WEDDING DRESS

"This one is gorgeous," I smiled with glee inside of the wedding boutique. Spinning around, displaying the Princess styled dress adorned with Organza. "When is the wedding," the owner asked. "Actually there isn't one. I was married once many years ago. I was 17 then with this being my first time actually wearing a wedding dress," I said simply.

Dumbfounded, the elderly owner asked, "what's the occasion?"

"Revenge."

My son's graduation was steadily approaching. Anthony had found us after being absent for 17 years. He got our address and began sending letters, begging for us to be together. I wasn't afraid, but it brought back all of the old feelings that I thought divorced freed me from. Some of his letters were cruel, threatening, and dark.

"You haven't seen the last of me," his letters read. Blood boiling to the point that I felt myself get sick with anxiety and posttraumatic stress, I decided to make sure if I did ever see him, it would be the last of him.

Taylor's graduation was a success. I thought I had evaded the possibility that he would show up, unannounced and unwelcome. My son was finally an adult and would be going to study abroad in Europe.

We fought the statistics of being survivors of domestic abuse and my teenage pregnancy. We were proof that statistics aren't applicable to all. It was time to start my life now that my son was starting his. I had a few loose strings to tie up before I could do that. Anthony was one of those haunting, damaged strings. Like a spider-web that you walked into, unaware, that sticks to you for moments after; it was time to trade places. He would become the prey for making me this way.

I got an email from Anthony saying that he was coming to Vegas and wanted to talk. I sent my phone number and we set a time.

"Meet me at the Dry Lake Bed. It's in Boulder City. Just outside of Las Vegas. I have a photo-shoot there. I'll have time to talk after," I told him.

Dusk had arrived; I pulled up to the dry desert lakebed, as dust followed my trail like smoke. Driving in a wedding gown was not easy, but I managed. The area was abandoned for miles.

Moments after, I saw Anthony. First time I had seen him since our divorce 17 years prior. I smiled at him and he nodded without emotion.

"Are you ready to apologize for ruining my life," Anthony asked.

"I did not ruin your life. YOU BEAT AND TORTURED A TEENAGER PREGNANT WITH YOUR CHILD," I screamed. Echoes bounced about the darkness.

The only lights were our headlights on our two vehicles nearby.

Anthony bit his bottom lip and balled up his fist, the same way he had many years ago. "APOLOGIZE TO ME," he yelled.

"Over my dead body," I whispered. Anthony then grabbed me by my hair. "Please stop," I begged. The demon is his eyes told me that he wasn't going to stop until I was dead.

I struggled a little bit before reaching into my bra and grabbing my taser. I placed it right on his neck as he collapsed motionless on the dusty ground. I leaned to the ground, and placed his face so he could see me. Temporarily paralyzed, I didn't have much time. His eyes reeked with surprise and a satisfying fear that excited me.

"I dressed up for this special occasion," I whispered. "Do you like my dress? I didn't get to wear one for you before. But I felt this was the right time."

I tased him once more to make sure he couldn't hop to his feet and defend himself.
"I wasn't strong enough then but I've grown a bit from that virgin you married and locked in the closet," I laughed.

I waited and watched as some of his muscles began to twitch. Then lifted my puffy wedding dress to reach the .40 Glock in the lace garter around my thigh.

Fired one shot into his leg and frightened myself at the power the gun held. "That one is for my son." Anthony began crawling away. It was fun to watch. "It's not so fun when the shoe is on the other foot now is it," I laughed maniacally.

Grabbing the taser out of my bra, I shocked him again. I leaned over, opened his mouth, placed the cold gun into his mouth, and whispered, "Apologize."

I took the gun out of his mouth and began gently sliding it across his face.

"I told you to leave me alone. You didn't listen. This one is for me."

BOOM.

I shot the finally round into his stomach. It was so loud that I couldn't hear anything but my heartbeat for a few moments. I went to my car, grabbed the kerosene, and lit his body on fire. His demons rose as the fire grew.
Like hell had met with Earth for this meeting. They danced atop him, screaming, and staring at me. I stared back into them and down at my bloody hands, finally free of him.

I dropped to my knees and prayed for forgiveness. If there was a God, he had to have mercy on me. The voices in my head began again. I grabbed my head, picturing Nuru the night at Disneyland when he did the same. Drowning out the voices with my favorite NIN's song, 'Kinda I want to," I drove back through the desert, bloody hands/dress, leaving the fiery mess in the distance.

COME TO ME...

CHAPTER: WATERFALL

It was raining pretty hard when I woke up. I could still taste the almonds and ahi tuna poke on my breath from last night's dinner. If you listened closely, the rhythm of the rain spoke in song.

"Come to me."

"You really shouldn't take that hike alone. It's dangerous," the gentleman at my rented house said. "I'm not afraid of anything," I smiled. "Alright tough guy, just be careful," he said closing the door.
Around 7am, I arrived my favorite mountains in Kaui'i. Adorned on my head was a flower crown made of fresh hibiscus. I began talking to Nuru.

"Answer me! You told me you would be here waiting for me if I came. I am here, "I screamed, feet emerged in the wet mud atop the mountain overlooking the sea.

Suddenly for the first time since he passed away, I saw him. He was dressed in red "flannel' and flip flops, with a smile so deep in his face you would see galaxies beyond. Hi smile was the smile with happy wrinkles that made his entire face light up. With Nuru's long mane blowing in the wind, I clasped his hand and looked over the cliff and we jumped…. Together this time.

So by now, you're wondering, was it really him? Was I communicating with his ghost or did my own demons cause me to do what I did. We all entertain shadows. We play with our monsters… we battle, and sometimes they win. Perhaps monsters are nothing more than an extension of our inner selves.

Helicopters were buzzing loud over the majestic Hawaiian terrain. The search party continued.

They never found my body.

But the shadows remain.

Be careful what you put up with. You become capable of doing whatever is repeatedly done to you. Enabling monsters will turn you into one.

About the Author

Khalilah Yasmin is an author and poet. She has her Bachelor of Science in Psychology. With a keen interest in human behavior, she enjoys the dichotomy between art and psychology as a medium to alter perceptions. Yasmin currently resides in Las Vegas, Nevada.

Twitter: @KhalilahYasmin
KhalilahYasmin.com